SEEKING
KOKOPELLI

SHELLEY MUNRO

Seeking Kokopelli

Print ISBN: 978-1-99-106322-9
Digital ISBN: 978-0-9951026-6-8

Cover: Kim Killion, The Killion Group Inc

Munro Press, New Zealand.

First Munro Press electronic publication November 2017

First Munro Press print publication March 2023

For Paul.

INTRODUCTION

Ever since Nate McKenzie hired on as a roadie, musician Adam James has lusted after him. So far Adam has kept his distance, knowing Nate is mourning his dead wife. But lately Adam has caught the man returning his stares. Maybe it's time to test the waters.

Besides, there isn't much chance Nate will find out that Adam was once his people's Kokopelli. His powers were stripped from him, along with the magical tattoo on his chest, when his orientation was discovered.

Nate is going crazy with guilt. Before his wife's death, he never looked at anyone else, woman or man. Now his dreams are filled with Adam. He tries to keep his mind on his job and off Adam's sexy body, but in a moment of weakness they share a kiss that sends them both up in flames.

Their relationship risks both their hearts and Adam's female fan base, but the attraction is too strong to ignore. Then someone takes a shot at Adam—and his tattoo begins to reappear, forcing him to come clean with his lover. And Nate must decide exactly where his future lies...before a killer steals it away from them.

This book contains rockin' music, smoky pubs, the mystical legend of Kokopelli and lots of playful, hot manlove.

PROLOGUE

LEGEND SAYS KOKOPELLI WAS a Native American fertility god, a prankster, a healer and a storyteller. He wandered from village to village in the Southwest of America, playing his flute and spreading his magic, bringing fruitful harvests and many new babies. He blessed the land and its people.

What most don't know is that the legend is true. Kokopelli lives on, the magic passed from son to son in the James family so the people and the land will thrive.

CHAPTER ONE

THE PLAINTIVE NOTES OF a sax throbbed through the gloomy pub. Nate McKenzie watched Adam James's strong fingers as he played, enthralled by both the performance and the man—a sexy, dark-haired figure illuminated in a golden spotlight. Adam caressed the music from his instrument, his eyes closed while he focused on playing the song.

Despite the other men and women in the crowded room, Nate felt as if Adam played for him. Only for him. Blood pounded through his veins, his cock drawing tight beneath the unforgiving denim of the faded jeans he wore. It was the same every time Adam played his saxophone or sang in that smoky voice of his. Intense arousal surged through Nate's mind along with confusion.

How could one man make him feel this way?

So lost. So incredibly aroused.

So damn needy.

Nate clenched his fingers around a bottle of beer and forced himself to take a sip. The warm taste of hops made him pull a face. *Rosa*. Thoughts of his wife should fill his mind, bring the sting of arousal to his cock and pull his body taut with desire, not his employer Adam James.

Sweet Jesus, Rosa hadn't been gone for that long. It was far too soon to try to fill the empty gap her death had left. His lips pressed tight. Both men and women might have interested him before he'd met his wife, but one look at her dark hair, flashing brown eyes, her curvy body, and he'd been smitten. He hadn't looked at another man since meeting Rosa.

Until Adam.

A pair of red lace panties sailed through the air and struck Adam's thigh before plopping to the stage. Adam continued playing smoothly as if nothing out of the ordinary had happened, filling the pub with his sultry, seductive music.

A woman screamed, "I love you, Adam."

The crowd roared. A few hooted with laughter. A second woman hollered an obscene suggestion of what she'd like to do if she cornered him alone.

5

Another pair of panties hit the stage. Nate turned away in disgust, telling himself it wasn't jealousy. He tipped back his head, swallowed the dregs of his beer and ordered another. His last one for the night, because he needed to make sure Adam and the other three members of Stampede made it back to their hotel rooms safely. He and Keith helped the band when they were on the road with security and anything else they required. Sometimes the women refused to let the band leave or, worse, tried to sneak into their vehicle or rooms.

Nate didn't expect problems tonight. This crowd appeared well behaved. They'd get the band back to the hotel. What the guys did after they reached the hotel was up to them. Nate's responsibilities for the night usually ended there.

Nate shot a quick look at Adam, took in the way the damp T-shirt clung to his chest and gulped. He saw a cold shower in his near future. And if that didn't work, he'd go for a run and take another icy shower when he returned. He would not think about Adam. He would not jerk off while thinking about the man again.

And no more spending time with Adam. If he followed these rules, maybe he'd manage to stuff the man into the 'friends box' instead of letting him drift into bloody uncharted territory. He was still faithful to Rosa, dammit.

It was way too soon to replace the memories he clutched close to his heart. And Adam—Adam had more women than he could possibly want. Why would Adam show interest in him?

The last haunting note of the sax drifted away, and the rest of the band joined in with the melody. Adam started to sing. His gaze drifted across the rapt audience and, although Nate knew Adam wouldn't be able to make him out in the gloom, the man seemed to stop looking when he glanced in his direction. Nate's breath caught in his throat. He stared at Adam's face, the intense eyes, the high cheekbones, the dark golden complexion. And that mouth...

A groan built deep in his throat. The man had him tied in knots and didn't even know it. Despite his growing fame, Adam was a private man. He handled his fans and the reporters with aplomb, hiding behind easy charm. They thought they knew him, but Nate looked deeper than most.

Adam James had secrets.

Nate didn't know what they were, didn't want to. A man deserved some privacy.

The song slid to an end, and the crowd burst into applause and cheers. Somewhere a woman hollered about her underwear, and Nate winced at her crudeness.

"Thanks," Adam said in a husky voice. "We're about to play our last song for the night. It's a new one for us. It's called 'Alone'."

The band started playing, with Adam singing the poignant lyrics about a man being alone, looking for love, a mate. The words tore at Nate's gut, ripping him open and laying his heart bare. He noticed a woman sitting not far from him with tears pouring unchecked down her cheeks.

Rosa. Damn, he missed her so much. She'd filled the empty loneliness inside him. It was almost one full year since she'd passed, and he missed her every single day, despite the weird yearning that struck him whenever he spent time near Adam.

Adam held the last note of the song, and the music trailed away. There was a long pause of pulsing silence before the cheering started. Nate couldn't help his pleased grin. Stampede had a new hit on their hands.

He stood, grabbed his Stetson off the bar and slapped it on his head before pushing his way through the crowd, holding his breath when a strong, heavy perfume hit him. He much preferred the honest scent of clean sweat. Soap. Some of these women needed to learn about subtlety.

Nate reached the stage at the same time as Keith, the other roadie. They were a small unit and worked well together. The two of them stood between the band and the crowd. Watching. Waiting while the band packed their equipment, ready to leave the stage and head for the rear entrance. Adam, Morgan, Cade and J.T., the men who made up Stampede, were pros and they worked efficiently together.

A couple of pub staff helped them and, fifteen minutes later, they were ready to depart for the hotel. A few women rushed outside, hoping to get autographs before the band left. The rest of the crowd stayed put to order more drinks and enjoy the evening. Someone dropped coins in the jukebox, and the notes of a country tune commenced with Shania informing the girls to get ready.

Nate breathed out a sigh of relief. It didn't always go easy like this. At the last place, the women had mobbed the band before they left the stage. He still bore a bruise on his ribs where a woman had jabbed him, using her elbows like weapons.

"Coming, Nate?" a voice called.

His heart skipped a beat when he realized it was Adam. "Yeah."

Adam stepped closer, his sensual lips stretched into a lopsided grin. "Are you bringing those with you?"

Nate followed Adam's gaze and a flush of heat flooded his cheeks. Shoot. He kicked the offending red panties off his boot. "Don't you get tired of getting pelted

9

with panties?" He'd bet half of them weren't even clean. Nothing surprised him anymore.

Adam shrugged. "Comes with the territory."

The reply did nothing to tamp down the weird jealousy streaking through Nate. Damn, what the hell was wrong with him lately? He glanced at Adam and away again, almost as quick. It seemed as if his mind had settled on one track, and that way led to Adam.

They slipped into silence, an edgy one on Nate's part, and exited the pub via the rear. As he'd expected, several women clamored for attention from the band.

"Do you want to sign autographs?" Nate wondered if Adam would accept one of the inevitable propositions that came with the territory. Hell! He forced the thought away. None of his business.

Adam smiled politely in the direction of the group of waiting women. "I'm tired, but I'll sign a few before we leave."

"Adam! Adam!" A petite woman with impossibly large boobs forced her way past Nate and thrust a marker pen at Adam. She glanced up at him coyly, fluttering her long mascara-laden lashes. "Sign my breasts for me."

"This is a permanent marker." A faint smile twitched at Adam's lips.

Although Adam wasn't talking to him, a shiver of

awareness pulsed across Nate's skin. Then the words sank in. The woman wanted Adam to touch her breasts. A growl escaped before he bit back his instinctive order for her to back off.

Not his place.

Adam chuckled. Nate wasn't sure if it was because of his reaction or the woman's request.

"I know," she cooed. "I don't want it to wash off too soon."

"Just as long as I don't get in trouble with the men in your life," Adam said as he uncapped the pen.

Nate turned away from them, glad of the hat and the dim light hiding his reaction to the situation. It was none of his business if Adam wanted to touch a woman. Hell, Adam could fuck her and it would still be none of his business.

He worked for Adam and Stampede. That was all.

THERE WAS SOMETHING ABOUT a long, slow seduction. Adam scrawled his signature across the top of the woman's breasts and handed back the pen with a wink.

"How about a kiss?"

"Sorry, sweetheart." Adam restrained a satisfied grin at

the second low growl behind him. "I don't want to get in trouble." He blew her a kiss and turned to the next woman waiting impatiently for an autograph.

While a slow seduction didn't have physical advantages, the furtive courtship he engaged in with Nate was the most fun he'd had in ages. Nate had started looking back. So far he hadn't registered Adam's pursuit, but he was interested. Confused too. Satisfaction pulsed through him at the secret knowledge.

After signing three more autographs, Adam waved to his fans and strode to the van. Nate walked directly behind him, and the devil in Adam made him halt abruptly. Nate crashed into his back. Seconds before he hit the ground, Nate grasped his hips, steadying him. Their bodies brushed before Nate stepped away, his hands falling from Adam's hips.

"Sorry. Thought I saw someone I knew." Adam caught his breath at the frisson of heat and climbed into the van before stupidity reared its head any further and he did something truly obvious. Nate followed and closed the door behind them. J.T. drove and, twenty minutes later, they pulled up outside their cheap hotel.

Morgan climbed out of the van, raising both tattooed arms into the air in a huge stretch. A groan vibrated in his throat before he spoke. "Man, I'm beat."

Cade smirked, his blue eyes sparkling with devilment. "Old man. I've got a date. I'll be late, so don't wait up."

"Me too." J.T. winked as he tugged the leather band from his dark brown hair. He ran a quick hand through his curls. "See you guys tomorrow at rehearsal."

Cade and Morgan both played guitar and did vocals while J.T. rocked big time with the drums. They'd started after Adam met Cade in a pub. Cade had introduced him to Morgan and J.T. and things had taken off from there with the band rapidly growing in popularity. They spent most of their time together. The band was his family now.

Morgan yawned. "What are you doing, Adam?"

"Gonna chill." Adam grabbed his saxophone. *And plan his next move with Nate.*

Nate and Keith drifted away with murmured good nights. Adam headed for his room, the one he shared with Cade. He'd intended to shower, grab a beer and blob in front of the box. Didn't happen. Restless energy filled him, and he couldn't sit still. Nate intruded again. Moodily, he kicked off his footwear. He'd never felt this way about a man before. There had been men over the years, clandestine sex that didn't mean a thing. This thing with Nate—it felt different.

Important.

He knew about Nate's marriage and his wife's

13

subsequent slow death from cancer. Hell, he knew it was too soon for Nate. The man still grieved. Despite the knowledge, he couldn't stop. Something inside him, something mystical, propelled him toward Nate, his gut telling Adam they'd be good together even though the man obviously preferred women. A sudden scowl formed. Heck, he was probably putting himself in the way of a shitload of hurt. His mind ordered him to walk away, but he couldn't. His heart ached to ferret out the possibilities.

Cursing softly, he grabbed a towel and his room key and strode past the row of rooms to the hot tub, wincing at the bite of gravel beneath his bare feet. Someone was already there when he arrived. About to retreat, he spied a familiar black Stetson sitting by the side of the tub. Nate.

"Great minds," Adam drawled, pitching his voice so it was audible above the bubble of the water. "Am I interrupting?"

Nate jackknifed to a sitting position. His mouth opened and closed before he sank under the surface again until only his head showed. The water plastered his dark hair to his skull. A faint dark mustache and light beard framed his mouth and chin. The rest of his face was cleanly shaven. Dark brown eyes glanced at him, then Nate averted his gaze. "Nah," he muttered finally. "Too wired to go to sleep yet."

"Me too." Adam yanked his black Stampede T-shirt over his head and shoved down his jeans. For propriety's sake, he left on his boxer-briefs before sliding into the warm water. They were both tall men and, for a brief second, their legs touched. Nate drew back like a startled cat.

"I won't bite." Adam kept his voice low and even. He'd like to do more than bite. He felt the surge in his body, the slight filling of his cock. Maybe this wasn't such a good idea. "And I don't have any nasty diseases."

Nate still refused to meet his gaze. "I'm not good company tonight."

"Problem?"

"Nothing I want to talk about."

Adam nodded. "Fair enough."

"Why aren't you with one of the women who throw themselves at you?"

Adam leaned back, letting the warm water work its magic. "Maybe I'm not interested."

"I guess it gets old fast." Nate frowned thoughtfully. "A man likes a challenge."

Yeah, the challenge thing worked for him. Time to kick up the pace in his seduction plan. "No." Adam watched Nate's face closely, needing to read him and his reaction clearly, if that was possible. "That's not what I meant."

Nate's brow furrowed. He sat up so his broad shoulders

and upper chest were visible. A light furring of dark hair covered his chest, arrowing downward beneath the water. "What do you mean?"

"Maybe I'm not interested in women."

The water stopped churning and stillness descended, interrupted only by the faint hum of traffic and the drone of a TV from the nearest guest room.

"You're gay?" Nate whispered, confusion and dismay on his face, a trace of panic.

Adam shrugged and leaned over to turn the timer on again. The water jets bubbled into motion, enveloping them in their own private world. He turned back to Nate. "I don't do labels."

"Why the hell are you telling me?" Nate sounded pissed now, and Adam wasn't sure why. "What the hell are you telling me?"

"I think of you as a friend."

"Man, I'm not that kind of a friend," Nate barked, his back straightening to military alertness, indignation snapping in his eyes.

Beneath the annoyance, Adam thought he caught a flash of heat. He wasn't sure what to make of it and sought to reassure. "Chill. We've known each other for almost a year. I haven't jumped you and I'm not about to." *Yet*. If Nate gave him some encouragement, that could change fast.

Adam had to work to control his impassive expression. No, he hadn't been wrong. He saw that flash of heat again. There was something there; otherwise, why would Nate sound so panicked?

Nate checked their surroundings before turning back to him. "Do the others know you're gay?"

"We've never discussed it."

"So why are you telling me? Women throw panties at you. They get you to sign their tits."

"What's your point?"

Nate shook his head, his throat moving as he swallowed. "I don't understand."

Adam wasn't sure he understood, either. Hopefully his instincts were right and he hadn't fucked up things between them, because he valued Nate's friendship. With Nate, he could be plain Adam James. He didn't have to perform. Play a part. He didn't have to live up to fans' expectations. Or conform to family pressure. "I think of you as my friend. Apart from the band, I don't have many friends. I wanted honesty between us."

"You're taking a risk, man. What happens if I tell the papers? Stampede is starting to take off. You're playing bigger venues now. Women and the whole panty thing is part of it all. If word gets out you're gay, you'll get a backlash. It'll hurt you, hurt the band."

All true, but Adam was sick of hiding. Besides, he had good intuition about people. Nate wasn't like that. They had a future together. Every instinct told him that, although he wasn't about to expose Nate to the family woo-woo shit. His gut feeling had served him well in the past, and he wasn't about to ignore it now.

"Tell me about your wife."

"Why?"

"Because I can see you're hurtin'. It's been almost a year."

"*No.*" The word was harsh, carried pain.

"Are you going to the rodeo tomorrow?" Adam smoothly changed the subject. One day Nate would talk. He could wait.

"Yeah, probably."

"I used to ride bulls when I was in high school."

"Yeah?" Interest flickered across Nate's face, replacing the previous panic. "You any good?"

"Nope." He grinned as he admitted the sad truth. "More enthusiasm than skill. I didn't make eight seconds more than twice the entire summer. Man, it was a rush, though. Like a drug. The cheers from the crowd. The music. The other guys egging you on. You do your prep, climb on top and when the chute opens, time seems to slow. Then the bull explodes out, solid muscle clasped between your thighs. The animal jumps, spins. It bucks and tries everything to toss you off. Yeah, I loved the rush." He grinned again in remembrance. "Although hittin' the hard ground wasn't so shit hot."

"Why did you stop?" Curiosity glinted in Nate, and the anxiety in Adam seeped away. Everything would work out between them.

"I met Cade and he introduced me to Morgan and J.T. We hit it off and formed Stampede. I didn't have time to do both music and rodeo."

"So now you sing about rodeos instead."

Adam chuckled. "Something like that, although we're not strictly a country band."

"Yeah, yeah. I've heard the official spiel." Nate leaned back, visibly relaxing, much to Adam's relief. "A blend of country and rock with a bit of blues tossed in."

"He listens." Adam stood and climbed from the pool. "I've had enough. Want to come back to my room for a drink before you hit the sack?" He knew his black boxer-briefs didn't leave much to the imagination and turned to grab his towel. Wrapping it around his waist, he glanced at Nate and caught him staring. Damn. Adam fought an inner battle, but his cock developed a mind of its own. He grabbed his discarded clothes and held them in front of him to hide his erection.

"I won't be good company."

"Doesn't matter." Adam wanted to continue their conversation. It didn't matter what they talked about. "I'll leave the door open for you." He walked away without looking back because he didn't want to give Nate a chance to wimp out.

He would not jerk off. Nate glared at Adam's departing back, wanting to call out and say he intended to go to bed. Alone.

Beneath the churning water, his cock rose, once again exerting a say on his actions. Guilt sliced his gut. This weird thing with Adam was killing him. He'd loved Rosa, he really had. But at the end she'd told him not to turn his back on a new love, that he had his whole future in front of him. Well, Nate didn't think she'd had a raging affair with another man in mind. She'd wanted him to find a good woman. Have children. Raise the family they'd always talked about. It wouldn't have occurred to her he might love a man, because they'd never discussed past lovers. It hadn't been an issue. He'd loved her, had never strayed or thought of another—male or female—while they were together.

Nate swore and surged from the water. For decency's sake, he wrapped a towel around his waist and tried not to think about Adam's fit, smooth body dripping wet from the tub. He tried not to think about the impressive male bulge, the tight ass and the tattoo that covered one shoulder. Nate dreamed about smoothing his tongue over the fancy whorls of that tattoo. Dreamed about it often.

He stomped back to his room, fumbling for the key. The door opened before he could fit the key to the lock.

"I'm heading to town. You want to come?" Keith, the other roadie, was a great guy. They worked well together.

"Nah, not tonight." Nate was grateful for the concealment of the clothes he carried. "I'm gonna crash. Have a couple of drinks for me."

He shut the door after Keith, glad to have the room to himself. That was one of the problems with being on the road all the time. The lack of privacy. It hadn't worried him at first. He'd needed the company after Rosa's death, but now, since the weird attraction to Adam, he craved solitude.

Nate padded to the bathroom and flipped on the shower. A hint of citrus aftershave and the lingering scent of soap filled the bathroom, telling him Keith had cleaned up before he left to go out on the town. Nate dropped his clothes and the towel on the tile floor before peeling off his navy blue swim trunks. His breath eased out with pure relief when his cock bobbed free.

When he stepped into the shower cubicle, the water sluiced over his tense shoulders and ran down his body. Nate sighed and picked up the soap. He dragged it over his chest and lower, scrubbing it over his groin. A slice of pleasure cut through him and, with a curse, Nate set the soap aside. Although he'd promised himself he wouldn't do this, he was in no condition to leave the room. He shouldn't stop by Adam's room, either. Knew it and intended to go anyway.

He fisted his cock, stroked, planting his feet firmly, and gave himself over to the pleasure. An intense burst of heat traveled the length of his body when he rubbed the bulbous head, palmed the sensitive underside. A couple more firm strokes, and he threw back his head, a moan of pleasure and Adam's name squeezing past his lips when orgasm took him. He continued stroking, milking himself until he had nothing left.

Heart pounding, he leaned weakly against the wall of the shower, the warm water still pouring over his body. Although he tried not to think about Adam, his mind went back to their conversation in the hot tub. Why had Adam confessed he was gay? And why hadn't Nate known?

Their manager probably had something to do with that. An older woman with a lot of business savvy, she'd crafted the band into a business package. The sexy image helped sell their music and pulled in the crowds at the intimate concerts they tended to play. Nate sensed the small gigs would become a thing of the past very soon because of the contract Stampede had signed two weeks ago. Susan wouldn't want anything to screw with that.

If it got out Adam was gay...

Nate stepped out of the shower to grab a towel and cussed. He was doing that a lot and knew Rosa wouldn't approve. Damn, he missed that woman, which made him an even bigger fool for thinking about Adam.

He pulled clean underwear, faded black jeans and a T-shirt out of his suitcase and dressed rapidly. This was a mistake. He knew it, but he still thrust his feet into a pair of Tevas, grabbed a bottle of whiskey from near his bed, and the key. Adam was right about one thing, and that was the only reason he was going for a drink. They were friends, and that's all they ever could be. Friends.

Somewhere in New Mexico

The man played the flute, the lilting notes hanging on the air before drifting away to be replaced by the next. A crowd gathered outside the open window of the faded

23

motel, listening to the music with grim expressions. One woman cried, tears streaming down her face. Another, heavily pregnant, held her belly in a protective manner.

The music ended abruptly, and the crowd dispersed with low murmurs. Several entered the rundown pub, the P of the illuminated sign no longer working. Others returned to their homes, seeking what pleasure they could in the comfort of familiar surroundings.

Three men remained, silently staring at the open window. Their well-patched clothes told of stretched budgets and unemployment. Their lined faces told of pain.

"Justin has lost his magic," one said, his gray hair pulled back in a long braid. "Kokopelli no longer favors him."

"The crops have failed for three years running. Hardly any of the women bloom and grow round with child," the youngest of the three said.

"I think we made a mistake," the third said. Lines underscored his eyes and bracketed his mouth. "We shouldn't have pushed Adam away, forced him to make a choice. We shouldn't have gone through with the ceremony and transferred the power of Kokopelli. We are being punished for our arrogance."

"We did what we thought was best," Gray Hair said. "We had no way of knowing the cost."

The youngest sighed. "Consequences. There is always

a price. We should have ignored our gut reactions, taken longer to consider before we stole Adam's powers and sent him away."

The third wrinkled his forehead, his shaggy brows meeting in a slashing line above his eyes. "What are we going to do to put things right? That is the question."

"I think we should find Adam and ask him to reconsider. Beg if we need to. The people need him, his magic," one said. "There must be some way to correct the mistake, some ceremony we can carry out to make things right."

The youngest nodded. "Yes. Yes. We must beg Adam's forgiveness and tell him we were too hasty. I will research for a way to make this happen."

Gray Hair sighed, a deep, tired sound. "And what if we can't change things? A second ceremony has never worked before. Maybe we should give Justin another chance?"

"We will find a way," the young one stated with a trace of defiance.

In the cheap motel room, the flutist gritted his teeth on hearing their murmured words, his hands clutching his instrument in a white-knuckle grip. He would go home and refuse to tour again. Let the people come to him if they wanted Kokopelli's help. That would work better, be more efficient, more enjoyable than putting up with seedy motels in one-horse villages. Decision made, Justin smiled. Then he noticed the ink stain on his hand and swore. Setting the flute aside, he rubbed the tattoo on his left pectoral muscle. His fingers came away covered with ink, and his heart pumped hard when he saw none of the original tattoo remained. It had vanished.

CHAPTER TWO

NATE HESITATED OUTSIDE ADAM'S room. His hand shook when he reached to push open the door. He closed his eyes for an instant; his breath eased out. Part of him knew crossing the threshold was a mistake. But he couldn't turn back, either, and have Adam draw incorrect conclusions. With a frustrated sigh, he cautiously stepped inside the room.

"I thought you'd decided not to have a drink with me. Grab a seat." Adam waved at one of the two queen-size beds. Black hair, damp at the ends from the spa pool, curled in disarray. His open shirt revealed a golden, muscular chest. "Do you want a beer or something stronger?"

"Stronger." Adam looked casual and too attractive for

Nate's peace of mind. Nate cursed under his breath, instant arousal jolting his dick to life again as he handed over his bottle of whiskey. He took a seat on the bed farthest away from Adam. Maybe the distance would help.

Adam cocked his head, staring at him before frowning. "You okay?"

"Ah...yeah." Nate had to clear his throat to force out the words. He was a fool for putting himself in this position. "Have you ever met anyone you wanted to have a long term relationship with?" And talking about *it* wasn't helping, blast it. He shifted uneasily on the bed, trying to find a comfortable spot.

"Yes." Adam handed him a glass holding a generous shot of whiskey before returning to get his drink.

Something about the other man's tone told Nate more than he wanted to know. "*Me?* Jesus, Adam. I'm a married man. Was a married man," he amended bleakly. "I like women."

"Don't get me wrong." Adam shrugged. "I like women, but men do it for me sexually."

"Not me." Nate's voice held a trace of defiance. He took a slug of whiskey, wincing at the burn across his tongue before he swallowed.

"Damn it, Nate. Stop behaving like I'm gonna jump you. I've never done anything out of line where you're concerned. I'm not about to start now."

"Good." Some of the tension residing in Nate's gut relaxed. "That's good."

Adam offered him a slow grin. "Unless you ask me to," he added.

Mid-swallow, Nate spluttered. Adam sauntered across the distance separating them and clapped him on the back. Not an improvement. The heat from his hand shot straight to Nate's groin. A groan escaped and he couldn't meet Adam's gaze.

"Damn, you're easy." Adam chuckled and stepped away to grab his guitar. "What do you think of this? It's a new song I'm working on."

Nate wanted to leave, except he knew that would be like sticking his head in the sand. Adam would know he was hiding and why. He'd have to tough it out for at least an hour, because the last thing he wanted was for Adam to realize how the smartass remarks unsettled him. Realizing his glass was empty, he stood and topped it up. He also poured more whiskey into Adam's glass before returning to sit on the bed.

For a while, he watched Adam, the way the man strummed his fingers across the guitar strings and the quiet joy on Adam's face as he played his instrument. When that became too much, Nate lay back and closed his eyes, listening to the music. There was no doubt Adam was a talented musician. The complete package. Fame had already come knocking at his door, and it wouldn't take long for him to become a household name.

Tired from several sleepless nights, Nate drifted off to sleep.

Adam drew the song to a close, smiling at his sleeping friend. He hadn't intended to lay out things quite as bluntly as he had, but Nate was still here. That had to be a good sign. For a few seconds, he thought about waking Nate, but decided to leave him. Adam set his guitar aside and flipped off the light, plunging the room into darkness. He stripped down to his boxer-briefs and crawled onto the bed. Even if Cade did return tonight, he wouldn't think anything of seeing them sharing a bed. They'd shared one room in some real dives during their time together, but if Cade caught them under intimate circumstances, then all bets were off.

Adam grinned. He didn't see that happening. He closed his eyes, realizing he was tired. The sound of Nate's breathing lulled him, and the last thing he remembered was smiling about the cuteness factor of Nate's snuffling.

Nate woke slowly, his erection cuddled up to a warm ass.

Remaining still, he breathed deep, drawing the familiar scent into his lungs. It was the best way to wake in the morning. With a contented sigh, he pressed closer.

"I never pegged you as a cuddler," Adam drawled.

Fully awake now, Nate jerked away with a heartfelt curse.

"Don't worry. I'm not going to tell anyone. Your secret's safe with me."

"Fuck, do you ever shut up?" Nate rolled off the bed and jumped to his feet, his heart pounding as if he'd run a hundred-meter sprint. "Why didn't you wake me?"

"You were tired. I didn't see the point of waking you. You want to go for a run?"

Nate scowled, his eyes narrowing while confusion pummeled him. "What are you trying to do to me?"

"Don't make too much of this," Adam said. "A run. That's all. We've run together before."

"I...yeah. Okay." Nate dragged a hand through his hair and turned toward the door, the desire to touch Adam throbbing through him like an aching tooth. "I'll grab my gear." He would not touch. He would not.

"Five minutes?"

"Yeah." Nate paused and strode back to Adam, his feet taking him even though his mind warned him of the big mistake he was about to make. He dragged Adam into his

31

arms and kissed him. Hard. Their noses mashed together. Teeth clacked before they managed a fit for their lips. The kiss was rough. Fierce and unrestrained. Nate cataloged the differences with part of his mind while he sank into the intimacy of being close to another person again. Adam's lips were soft, but the contrasting rasp of stubble made the kiss different. The hard body rubbing against his own was different as well, with none of the cushioning curves he'd enjoyed with Rosa.

Rosa.

He wrenched from Adam's arms and hurried to the door, yanking it open. His breath came in loud gasps, almost panicked. "There. No big deal. It's over and now we both know."

"Know what?" Adam padded up behind him and pushed his hand against the door. It shut with a sharp click. "What do we know?"

"That we don't work together. We're plain wrong." Nate stared at the paintwork of the door, tried to ignore the note of panic in his voice, but he knew it was there. So did Adam. And the blood crowding his cock didn't lie, either. He wanted more.

"Practice makes perfect," Adam whispered close to his ear, placing one hand on either side of his body and effectively caging him against the door. "Turn around."

Nate swallowed. He could feel Adam's body along his back, the heat of him. Smell him—clean, musky male. Damn, he couldn't show fear. He had to bluff his way out of this, pretend the kiss hadn't made him crazy and backfired on him. Instead of disgust, he wanted to explore Adam's body. Worse, he wanted to kiss and touch every inch.

Who'd have thought a single kiss would cause so much trouble. He should have walked away instead of following his stupid impulse to try to prove to Adam he was wrong about an attraction between them.

"I wouldn't have taken you for a coward."

Indignant, Nate turned to glare at Adam. "I'm not a cow—"

Adam stopped his heated words with a kiss. This one, it was nothing like the first. It started slow, a mere brushing of lips, the gentleness of it sending signal fires darting through Nate's body. He gasped, and Adam took advantage, stroking his tongue over Nate's, deepening the contact. Adam didn't move, didn't do anything except kiss him.

Somewhere along the line, Nate forgot he was kissing a man and went with the soar of sensations racing through him, the pleasure. The yearning.

Slowly, Adam pulled away, and Nate realized he gripped

the other man's shoulders. He snatched his hands away, a tide of embarrassment spreading across his cheeks. That couldn't happen again, which was a shame because he'd enjoyed the kiss. Innate honesty made him admit it to himself, and the fact that he wanted more. And worst of all, he'd never thought of Rosa the entire time.

"We'll get even better with time," Adam whispered.

"There won't be another time." Maybe if he said it enough, he'd come to believe it.

"No? I didn't take you for a liar, either."

"Fuck, will you stop touching me?" Fury sped through Nate, and he shoved Adam, his hands curling to fists at his sides. "I thought you wanted to run."

"Whatever." Frustration shaded Adam's voice this time. He stepped away to sit on the corner of the bed. "But remember this. No matter how hard and fast you run, you can't outrun the truth."

Nate opened his mouth, about to tell Adam where to shove his truth. Something made him bite back the words, and he jerked the door open, then stomped outside.

"Five minutes," Adam called after him.

Nate strode to his room and used his key to open the door. It was light out, but with the lack of noise and bustle that characterized the early hour. Perfect for a run. Snorting, he pushed inside the room. Once he realized Keith had returned and was still asleep, he made a conscious attempt to keep the noise down. Even knowing he should stay far away from Adam, Nate rifled through his bag for a pair of shorts and a tank top. Rapidly stripping, he ignored his hard-on and dressed for running.

Adam was right. He couldn't run away, not when their lives and work intertwined so intimately. But he could ignore the man and the traitorous feelings that zapped him each time they were together. Nate laced his shoes and, after shoving the key in the zip pocket of his shorts, walked outside.

Adam was waiting, already working through a series of stretches. Nate joined him and commenced his own stretching routine. Neither man spoke. Somehow that was worse than discussing the topic sitting like a ten-ton elephant between them.

"Where do you want to run?" Nate's words were a husky growl. Damn. That wasn't the impression he wanted to give. He felt Adam's gaze stroke his face, drop briefly to his lips, and Nate uneasily shifted his weight from one foot to the other.

"Why don't we head for the forest reserve?"

Nate's head jerked up at the suggestion. "That's a long run." Adam wasn't as fit as him. The run would challenge him.

Adam shrugged. "I need a good workout."

Nate skewered him with a sharp look even as he stiffened at the suggestion buried in Adam's words. "Let's go." He started running, taking the lead because the more of Adam he saw, the bigger his erection grew. Running was gonna hurt like hell, although the alternative didn't work for him, either.

"Stop thinking so hard," Adam mocked, running easily at his side.

"One of us has to think straight."

"Why? What's so wrong about spending time with people you like? Because that's what it comes down to."

Nate upped the pace a bit, hoping Adam would tire. Didn't happen, and he slowed again to an easy pace, one he knew they could sustain all the way to the reserve. "This is a bad idea."

"Why?" Adam demanded again. "Spell it out. Give me reasons and maybe I'll agree."

"First there's the fact that I'm not gay," Nate said in a hard voice, shooting Adam a quick glance before returning his attention to the road in front of them.

"I never said you were."

"I'm not over Rosa yet. I miss her."

"Of course you do. I'm not lookin' to replace Rosa. I didn't know her, but if she was important to you, then she was a good woman."

Nate's steps faltered before he picked up the smooth pace again. He'd started working for Stampede after Rosa saw the job in a local paper. She'd told him he needed employment, he'd need friends after she died, and she thought this would be a good job for him. He hadn't wanted to leave her to go to the interview, hadn't wanted to take the job when Stampede's manager had offered it to him. Rosa had insisted, saying he needed this particular job. Nate hadn't had the heart to tell Rosa no, and he'd started working for Stampede. When Rosa had died, they'd been there for him and had become family. That's what made his feelings for Adam so difficult. Stampede was like a last contact to Rosa.

If he left and terminated his contact with Adam and Stampede, he didn't think he'd survive. The last thing he wanted was to slide back into alcohol like he had straight after Rosa's death. And he could see it would be easy to fall into that trap with nothing to fill his days.

"I miss her like hell." Tears stung the back of his eyes at the admission. He wished she were still here. He could have talked to her. She would have known what to do about Adam. Even though she hadn't known about the men before her, she wouldn't have judged him. Rosa had been like that—fair-minded with a big heart.

"Of course you do. No one wants to replace Rosa. She'll always be a part of you." Adam's words were strained, his breathing hard from the exertion of the run.

Nate slowed a fraction more. "I can't remember her face. I look at photos, but I'm losing memories. She doesn't deserve that." His breath caught as he admitted his fears. He couldn't believe he'd actually told Adam his dark secret. What the hell kind of person couldn't remember what his wife looked like, smelled like?

Adam stopped abruptly, and Nate slowed, turning to look over his shoulder.

"I need to walk for a bit."

Nate stopped and waited for Adam to catch up. If Adam started blathering about Rosa, he was gonna start running again.

"What else?" Adam demanded. "What are your other reasons?" Sweat coated his shoulders and arms, his face. He was a bit shorter than Nate but kept in shape, hitting the gym when the opportunity presented itself. The band often played basketball during breaks, and Nate and Keith joined them. Nate wondered what it was like for Adam, being gay and having to keep it hidden. When he thought about it, he'd never heard Adam mouth off about his lovers like some of the others.

"You can't have a male lover, not publicly."

"I've always had male lovers. I choose not to talk about them or make the fact public. I'm a private man."

"So you're willing to stay in the closet?"

"If my lover wanted me to come out, I would, if he were important to me. I'm not hiding because I'm scared of what other people think."

Nate scowled, catching the underlying message. If he wanted Adam to come out, if he wanted an open relationship, then he'd do it. Nate had a couple of problems with that. One, he wasn't interested. And two, he didn't want to live under a public spotlight. "I don't know why you're telling me. I don't care one way or the other. You ready to run again?"

Adam picked his pace up into a jog. "I'm telling you because you're my friend. What else?"

"I want to have kids. I've always wanted to have kids."

"So why didn't you and Rosa have children straight away?"

"Rosa wanted to. I put her off," Nate said. "I wanted kids, but I thought we should have time together first, then Rosa got sick."

"Anything else?"

Huh! Nothing to refute with the children argument. Two guys together could adopt children these days, but it wasn't an easy road, not with the prejudice regarding gays.

39

Not that he was gay.

"I like women, the way they feel. Their softness and the way they smell."

"All good arguments," Adam said.

The entrance to the forest reserve was up ahead. They ran through the gateway and turned onto the dirt track leading to a reservoir. Behind them, a car slowed and turned in behind them before driving to the parking area. Nate kept running, the scent of pine filling each inhalation. The path grew steeper and they could no longer run abreast of each other. Adam dropped back, and Nate could hear each gasping breath the other man took. He became ultra-aware of him and imagined Adam staring at his body—his back and ass.

His mind drifted back to the kiss. The second one. He'd never admit it to Adam, but he'd enjoyed it, had liked feeling Adam's hands touching him. Not that he'd allow it to happen again. No, tonight he'd go to a bar. Find a woman to chat with and take things from there. His conscience took a hit at the decision, and he shoved the guilt aside. As Adam pointed out, Rosa was gone. Sometimes a man needed more than his hand.

Up ahead, Nate caught the glint of the water through the trees. The incline smoothed out to level and, despite the sweat coating his body, he was glad he'd joined Adam today. The run had settled his mind and helped him come to a decision.

Nate ran until he hit the water's edge. He stopped when he heard Adam's labored breathing and started doing stretches, grinning at the other man as he approached.

"How are you feeling?"

"Shattered," Adam said dryly, still breathing hard. "I shouldn't have suggested a run after such a late night." He did a couple of halfhearted stretches before flinging himself on the ground with a loud groan. Over the other side of the lake, three deer darted away, disturbed by the noise. They crashed through the undergrowth, disappearing into the trees.

Nate chuckled and dropped to the ground beside him. The early morning sun felt good and not too hot. That would come later in the day. "We could have sat and watched them if you hadn't made so much noise."

"There are lots of deer around here. We've seen them near the hotel before. They graze next door to the rodeo grounds sometimes." Adam paused to wipe the sweat from his forehead with the hem of his T-shirt. "You didn't mention the kissing on your list," he said suddenly.

With good reason. That kiss… "I don't wanna talk about it."

"Avoidance," Adam said.

Nate turned to glare. "Why are you pushing me?"

"Because you think of me as more than a friend, but you're too scared to admit it. You're frightened of what I make you feel."

"You have no idea what I feel. And what the fuck are you talking about feelings for, anyway? I don't talk about that crap, and I'm not about to start with you."

"Could have fooled me." Adam sounded amused. "I've learned a lot about you this morning. Besides, if you hate talking to me that much, all you need to do is tell me to piss off."

"What? It's that simple?"

"Yeah."

"Piss off."

"I didn't say I'd listen." Adam's grin reminded Nate of a small kid's with the way it lit up his features. He put his whole heart into his smile.

Nate snorted and tried not to react to the boyish grin. "Yeah, that's what I thought."

"Go on." Adam closed the distance between them. "You know you like me."

"Piss off." Nate wanted to leap to his feet and step away, but his body wouldn't obey.

"Hey, you started this by kissing me first."

All true. Nate's eyes slid closed, a groan of despair

building inside him. He shouldn't want this. Obviously, he needed to get laid. He needed to find a woman to help clear his mind, rid himself of this confusion. Then he felt Adam close the distance between them. Before he could protest, Adam's lips settled on his, driving the thought from his head. Adam's mouth was whisper-soft, cajoling rather than demanding, and it was this gentleness that broke through his reserve. A growl rumbled from his throat, but it wasn't one of dissent. In his heart, Nate knew a turning point when he experienced one. Fear grabbed him for an instant before the heat of Adam's mouth stole away his anxiety.

Their lips moved together without haste as they tasted and learned each other. Apart from their lips, they didn't touch, but Nate could feel the warmth coming off Adam's sweaty body and the heat generated by his own.

Adam licked along the seam of his lips, silently encouraging him to open. Nate obeyed, accepting a passive role because he couldn't fight the other man and the rioting emotions inside him as well. Adam sucked on his tongue, moving nearer to wrap his arms around Nate's shoulders, tugging him close and lying back so they sprawled full length on the ground. Their erections brushed, and a frisson of heat struck Nate hard. His entire body jerked.

Adam lifted his head. "Something wrong?" The twinkle in his eyes told Nate he knew despite asking the question.

Nate stared, refusing to answer because everything he said landed him deeper in trouble. His inner battle died with a pitiful whimper.

"I didn't think so." Adam's tone was smug. "Kiss me again."

Although Nate wanted to refuse, he couldn't. He tried to draw a picture of Rosa in his head. Her beautiful features were fuzzy, her smile distant, as if she'd moved on, leaving him behind.

"Kiss me, Nate."

Nate got it. Adam refused to let him hide. If they continued, it would be because he'd initiated the kiss. Cursing softly at his weakness, he leaned in and brushed a kiss on Adam's jaw, the stubble rough but somehow stimulating. Nate closed his eyes and went with instinct, kissing Adam exactly the way Nate liked. He trailed kisses along Adam's jawline and down his neck, tasting the saltiness of his skin. He didn't let himself think, just went with the magic building between them. Adam gripped his shoulders, breathing hard and starting when Nate nipped him.

"Damn, that feels good. Do it again."

Nate jerked away from Adam, the spell broken by

Adam's words. "I...I..."

Adam placed his fingers across Nate's mouth. "It's okay. We can take this as slow as you want. We have plenty of time."

JUSTIN JAMES WATCHED THE two queers kissing, disgust welling up from the pit of his stomach. Things never changed. His younger brother was still gay. And they wanted to find Adam, ask him to return to the village. He spat in disgust, cheering inwardly when the globule hit an insect. Distracted for an instant, he watched the tiny insect struggle, not looking back at the two men until the bug stilled.

They were still kissing.

A wave of hate swept him. Because of Adam, he'd started life at a disadvantage. Kokopelli should have automatically come to him, formed the distinctive tattoo on his chest. Instead, the powers had ignored him to reward his younger brother. And now...now Adam threatened to destroy everything he'd fought for, everything he'd earned. If Adam returned, he'd lose his job as Kokopelli, his power, his position in the village—if his father and the elders had their way and reinstated Adam somehow.

His reputation.

He'd lose his livelihood and the perks that came with it—the women, the money. The prestige of holding Kokopelli's powers.

No, Adam couldn't return to the village to take his place.

Lucky he'd kept tabs on his brother and knew where to find him. He'd followed Adam's progress, a small part of him proud of his brother's achievements when he knew Adam had left with nothing more than the clothes on his back and his guitar.

Funny, the guitar that had caused so much strife and consternation amongst the followers was the one thing that had saved Adam. No matter how often they punished his brother, Adam had refused to give up the instrument in favor of the flute. He'd never seen Adam play a flute since the last big argument. His kid brother did play a mean saxophone, though.

His mouth pursed when the two men clutched each other, moving indecently close. The few good memories jolted free, fading under the weight of his disapproval. The two men kissed as if they were the only people in the world. Even though he wanted to, he couldn't look away. To his discomfort, it was kinda hot watching their lack of restraint, and obvious pleasure and guilt started to displace the disgust.

He shook his head, wishing there was another way, but he'd thought long and hard during the drive to Cody.

Adam had to die.

Justin stooped to open the bag he'd tossed on the ground at his feet and pulled out the rifle. A sliver of sorrow pierced his conscience for a second until he thrust it away and aimed.

He was sorry, but some things a man couldn't change.

ADAM DROWNED IN SENSATIONS. Sexual frustration tore at his gut, his cock and balls so damn tight they throbbed. He hadn't felt like this in a long time and relished the experience, despite the pain. This thing with Nate, it was right. But he wouldn't push the other man for more than he was willing to give. He still mourned Rosa. Adam forced away his jealousy, consigning it to the far reaches of his mind. A clear head. That's what he needed now. And patience. Nate was as skittish as a newborn colt.

He knew one thing: The man could kiss. He wondered how Nate's mouth would feel sucking on his cock, and almost lost it. Pushing away and breathing hard, he put a little distance between their lower bodies while still maintaining his grip on Nate's shoulders. He didn't want

Nate to move his hips at the wrong time and push him over the edge. Somehow he didn't think Nate was ready for that yet. "We should get back to the motel. I don't wanna be late for rehearsal."

"Yeah, okay." Nate blinked, the dreamy lust fading from his eyes, the familiar wariness returning.

Not good timing, but he refused to let down the rest of the band. Despite late nights and possible hangovers, Adam knew they'd turn up for rehearsal. "One last kiss."

Nate didn't move. He just stared at him.

"Go on. One little kiss."

"You are a pain in the ass."

The comeback was on Adam's lips before the thought even formed. "I could be your pain in the ass." The words hung between them, and Adam noticed the slow rise of color in Nate's cheeks. "I'm sorry. I—"

A shot rang out, echoing across the lake. A bird shrieked in alarm. A second shot fired, a piece of bark hitting Adam on the cheek.

Nate grabbed Adam as a third shot rang out. Adam felt a searing pain on his right biceps before he rolled with Nate's solid body covering him. The undergrowth was sparse, but the dip they'd fallen into helped to cover them. He caught a whiff of pine and the rich scent of soil along with masculine sweat. Damn, his arm throbbed. He tried to move it and decided there wasn't much damage, although it would hurt when he tried to play his sax.

"You okay?"

"I'd be more okay if we were naked." Adam held his breath when he heard Nate's sharp inhalation. Despite the pain in his arm, he wanted to laugh.

"You're bleeding. No, stay down. They might shoot again."

"I thought this was a reserve with no hunting allowed."

In the distance, they heard a vehicle start and leave with a roar of the engine.

He sensed Nate's shrug rather than saw it. "Times are tough." Nate shifted a fraction and stuck his head up to scan the area. "People try to make ends meet where they can, even if that means illegal hunting."

Adam snorted. "You're wearing yellow. My T-shirt is bright blue. If they think we're deer, they need their eyes checked. Do you think that was them leaving?"

An SUV pulled up in the small parking area.

"Maybe they were scared off." Nate squinted into the sun. "It's a man and woman with three kids."

Adam started to stand, but Nate pushed him back down. Adam fought him off and stood. "Those kids are making enough noise to scare the animals at Yellowstone."

"Shit, you're bleeding more than I thought."

49

Adam scowled at the blood trickling down his arm and looked away. As a matter of principle, he tried not to think too much about the color and scent of his blood. Sometimes the sight made him woozy, and the last thing he wanted to do was faint. Before he could steel himself to investigate his wound, Nate pushed his hand away. "Let me."

Nate cared. Adam could see it in the wrinkle of his brow and the unguarded expression in his eyes. It made him want to smile, to tease, and it definitely took his mind off the bright red of the blood.

"Does it hurt?"

"A bit," Adam said. "It's bearable."

Nate inspected it again. "It's just a graze." He dragged his tank top over his head and ripped it up. "Not exactly hygienic, but we need to stop your bleeding." He pressed one piece against the wound and wrapped a second piece around, tying it in place. "I don't think you'll need a doctor, as long as it doesn't get infected. We can clean it up properly when we get to the motel."

"Assuming I can run back."

"Aw, hell. I wasn't thinking. I'll run back and grab a vehicle."

Adam laughed out loud this time. "I'm fine. It stings a bit. That's all. I can run. I'm not going to be late to rehearsal and have the guys rib me. Besides, I'm not sure I can afford to pay the beer and pizza fine for being late. We run."

"And what if the gunman is still around?"

"If he is, he'd be stupid. There's another car full of kids. It's not exactly quiet now. Besides, the deer have disappeared. His was probably the vehicle we heard leaving in a hurry. We should report it, though. Someone might get really hurt next time."

Nate stood and scanned their surroundings. "I can't see any bullets."

"The bullets could have gone anywhere. I didn't even see which direction the shots came from."

"Are you sure you're up to running back?"

"I don't need a nursemaid. That's not what I'm looking for from you."

Instantly, awareness surged between them. Nate avoided his gaze, and Adam smirked. Ripe for the picking. Nate belonged to him. The man just didn't realize it yet.

"You're late," Cade said when Adam and Nate walked into the pub they were playing the following night.

"We had to stop in to see the sheriff." Nate's breath eased

out only when he realized none of the men were treating him any differently from normal. "Adam and I went for a run out to the reservoir and someone shot at us."

"And we had to doctor my arm. The idiot almost got me good," Adam said, indicating the snowy bandage on his right arm.

As a distraction, it was a pretty good one. Nate didn't think any of their friends would suspect the pair of them had been in a lip-lock seconds before the hunter shot at them.

CHAPTER THREE

ADAM PULLED OUT HIS guitar, falling into rehearsal mode with Cade, J.T. and Morgan. Soon, music filled the room. Nate listened for a while before joining Keith. They hauled equipment from the van into the pub, storing it for the following night in a secure room, sorted out lighting and went through their usual before-show routine, discussing security and potential problems.

Nate moved on autopilot, his mind drifting back to kissing Adam. He wanted to tell himself he'd hated Adam touching him, but that would be a big fat lie.

So what did this mean?

Man, he couldn't imagine a relationship with Adam going over well with his parents and two older brothers. A relationship with any man. Nate took off his hat and dragged a hand through his hair before settling the black Stetson back on his head. Nah, there were too many potential problems if he let things with Adam progress further. Eventually, he wanted children. Besides, he liked women. Their softness. The way they laughed. The way they smelled so fine. A small, traitorous voice in his head reminded him Adam had felt good in his arms.

Different. Nate's shoulders slumped as he admitted the truth. Not bad...different. Different wasn't bad. Nate squashed the furtive thought immediately.

Adam...

Nate spat out a curse, cringing inwardly because he knew if Rosa were watching from heaven she'd make an annoying tsking sound at the back of her throat. As the thought occurred, he realized with embarrassment that if Rosa had heard his curse, she'd probably seen him with Adam. That settled it.

He would not mess around with Adam again.

HE'D MISSED. JUSTIN BLINKED, recalling the moment of pulling the trigger, the pressure of his finger against the unforgiving metal. The moment of doubt and denial. *Guilt.* His hand had trembled, and he'd missed. The second shot had gone wild too.

Then he'd heard a vehicle approaching. He'd risked a third shot and run for his SUV, driving away from the reserve at a reasonable speed when every instinct had screamed in panic, telling him to floor the accelerator.

He hadn't thought it would be so hard to pull the trigger, to fire a bullet into his brother. A keen hunter, he'd always managed to land his prey. He'd tried to think of Adam as prey. It hadn't worked.

Justin paced, his dark hair swinging around his face. He swiped at it impatiently before striding to the bathroom of the motel room and grabbing his brush. With practiced ease, he dragged the bristles through his hair and tied it back with a leather strap.

He'd learned something about himself today. A conscience. He still had one. He supposed the knowledge should make him feel better. It didn't. Instead, a sick, almost desperate sensation squirmed through the pit of his stomach. It was too late for scruples.

Move on to the next plan.

He couldn't afford to let Adam live. The alternative...

No! Justin shivered and reached for the prepaid phone he'd purchased the previous day. Onward and upward. Adam would die, and Justin's life would revert to normal without this specter hanging over him, because without the Kokopelli mantle he was nothing. An unemployed has-been. He winced as possible consequences slapped him in the face. Lara would walk. A harsh intake of breath cut through the silence, along with a slice of fear.

He couldn't let that happen.

"WELCOME TO THE CODY Nite Rodeo!"

Adam hooted and whistled along with the rest of the band. The entire crew had come to the rodeo tonight, including Nate. Glancing along the row where he and the rest of the band sat, Adam looked at Nate. His ever-present Stetson shaded his face and kept Adam from seeing his expression. The man was avoiding him and had purposely sat miles away from him with Cade, J.T., Keith and Morgan separating them. Adam grinned, knowing he would have misbehaved. He wouldn't have been able to resist touching and teasing Nate, so it was a wise move on Nate's part.

Music blared from the loudspeakers, dragging his attention from Nate. Horses and riders tore around the ring, bearing flags from the countries involved in rodeo. The flags fluttered and snapped in the breeze, streaming behind them, their appearance heightening the crowd's anticipation for the events to come.

Adam settled back to enjoy the show. Nate would keep. At least the man had attended the rodeo. He could have excused himself and done his own thing.

The first bareback rider catapulted from the chutes on a horse called Hellfire. Two seconds later, rider and horse parted company, the crowd erupting with cheers and sympathy when the rider rose slowly to his feet and hobbled away.

"Man, that must have hurt," Morgan said.

Cade chuckled, shaking his head. "Rather him than me."

"I used to ride the horses when I was younger and stupid," J.T. commented.

Morgan smirked. "You're still stupid."

J.T. lifted a finger in a rude salute while the rest of the band chortled.

Adam grinned openly. "I used to ride bulls. I was also younger. Never stupid, though. I stopped riding, didn't I?"

"Did you fall on your head?" Keith asked.

"Broke my leg," Adam said. "That was when the stupid part of me escaped, and I concentrated on guitar and started writing songs. And I met Cade, who talked me into joining his band."

SHELLEY MUNRO

"Huh, he fell on his head," Cade said. "He turned down a date with that chick last night, the one who said she was Miss Rodeo Wyoming."

"She only wanted me for my body." Adam shrugged without apology. "Who wants to end up as a notch on some woman's bedpost? I like to do my own picking."

"And he's fussy about it," Nate said, his eyes glittering with challenge as he glanced down the row. "He hardly ever dates."

Adam winked at Nate and took pleasure in the other man's startled expression, the way he turned away to study the arena. They both knew why he didn't date women. Nate knew who he wanted in his bed, and that was enough for Adam. The next move was up to Nate.

"You turned her down? Man, Adam, that babe was stacked. She can have my body any time," Cade said.

Adam shook his head in mock sorrow. "Easy. You're so easy it's scary."

"Nate's right. You hardly ever go out," Morgan said. "The babes throw themselves at you at every gig."

"Nah, it's the panties they throw," Adam said. "I go on dates. I like to keep that part of my life private."

Nate shot him a defiant look. "Have you got a secret lover, Adam?"

J.T. slapped Nate across the back, chuckling while

watching another cowboy part company from his horse. "Good one, mate. That's what I want to know."

Adam scowled. "None of your business."

"Check out his expression," Cade said, laughing, and they all studied him, curiosity burning their faces.

"Anyone want a beer?" Adam asked.

A horse burst from the chutes, bucking and twisting, with the cowboy raking his spurs yet clinging at the same time. The buzzer went eight long seconds later, and the pickup riders galloped after the bronco, then dragged the cowboy off to safety.

"That's the first clear round of the night for Austin Maxwell," the announcer called over the loudspeakers. Music blared and the crowd applauded.

Adam stood. "Beer?" he asked again.

"I'll help," Cade said, following him when everyone said they wanted one.

They fell into step after clearing the stands, making their way around the back to where one of the sponsors had set up shop.

"Do you have someone?" Cade asked, serious now that he was away from the rest of the band.

Adam thought about Nate. "Yes," he said. "There's someone."

"Someone at home?"

Adam shrugged, hoping Cade would make his own assumptions. He would never out Nate like that or open him to ridicule. Part of him even understood why Nate was being so confrontational tonight. A slow smile bloomed inside, curling his lips upward. He had Nate running scared. The knowledge made him think of all kinds of decadent pleasures, things he could experience with Nate.

"It's hard being on the road," Cade said. "I couldn't do a long-distance relationship."

"I'll take six beers," Adam said to the guy behind the bar. He pulled out his wallet and handed over several notes.

Someone crowded them from behind, pushing to get to the counter.

"Back off," Cade growled, glaring at the three men standing behind them.

Adam turned, nailing them with a hard look. Neither he nor Cade was a small man, but the three idiots glowered back and muttered a string of curses.

"Hey, we don't want any problems here," the guy behind the bar said.

"Let's go," Cade said, picking up a tray of beers. "I've no idea what put a bug up their asses."

They arrived back at the stands without trouble, although Adam's gut rumbled with warning, and he kept glancing over his shoulder. He trusted his instincts. Always had, which was why he was paying attention to the prickle at the back of his neck now.

The rodeo program ran smoothly, progressing through the calf roping, the barrel racing and the antics of the clowns or bullfighters, the title they preferred these days. The final event on the program was the bull riding.

Adam watched closely, his past experience allowing him to study the rides and judge where the cowboys came unglued. It was usually their failure to compensate for a change of direction in spin from the bull, loss of focus or incorrect positioning that sent them hurtling to the ground.

"Here comes Tad Green riding Big Bad Brown." The announcer ran through the bull's stats and Tad's riding percentage. "This bull has only been ridden once. He has a ninety-five percent buck-off rate."

The bull jumped from the chute when the gate opened, skipping once before settling into a clockwise spin. Adam held his breath, almost feeling the pull of gravity on his body, the jerky whiplash firing up his spine. The bull straightened, then whipped into a spin in the opposite direction, taking the cowboy by surprise. He flew through the air and hit the ground with a jolt. Adam winced, heard the hiss of breath through Cade's teeth.

The two bullfighters stepped in, diverting the bull's

attention from the fallen cowboy. The man scrambled to his feet and retrieved his hat and bull rope before leaving the ring to the applause of the crowd.

"No ride for Tad Green," the announcer said.

"Mad," Cade said with a shake of his head.

Adam grinned. "Don't you know cowboys score?"

"Is that why you rode bulls?"

"Yep." Although he scored with other cowboys, not that he intended to introduce this snippet to the conversation. He had fond memories of his first lover—a guy who rode saddle broncs and roped on the side. Adam had heard he'd retired to run a successful ranch in Missouri.

The bull riding event progressed quickly and, half an hour later, the crowd around them started to leave the stands.

"Anyone for a drink in town?" J.T. asked.

Adam shook his head. "Nah, I'm beat and my arm is throbbing. I'm going to walk back to the motel."

"I have another date," Cade said with a smirk. "I'll walk back with you. I want to change before I head out. Don't expect me until late morning."

"One word for you," Morgan said. "Condoms."

"Don't worry. My little soldiers are well trained. They don't venture places they shouldn't."

"Hell," Adam said, clapping his hands over his ears. "I

don't wanna hear that stuff. Puts all sorts of visions in my head."

J.T. laughed. "Cade, that's good to hear. We won't have to worry about any shotgun-toting fathers chasing us at our gigs."

They stood and moved with the crowd to the exit.

"Are you guys sure you wanna walk?" J.T. asked.

"It's not far," Cade said, striding in the direction of the path that led from the rodeo grounds to the hotels and businesses farther down the road.

Adam followed Cade with a wave at the others. By the time they organized themselves and climbed in the van plus fought the traffic streaming from the grounds, he and Cade would be halfway back to the motel.

They walked along the gravel path, leaving the bustle of the rodeo behind. The path ran along the edge of a reserve and, once they left the floodlit area, Adam's night vision kicked in.

"Damn, it's dark out here," Cade muttered. "Spooky."

Adam noticed he glanced over his shoulder in the direction of the rodeo grounds a couple of times with a frown.

"Did you hear that?"

"Someone else is walking behind us," Adam said, keeping his voice matter-of-fact even though his gut

63

jumped with a preternatural awareness. He upped his pace, lengthening his strides, scowling at the rapid footsteps echoing behind.

Without further warning, the same men who'd hassled them at the beer stand rushed from the darkness.

Cade groaned. "Aw, crap. If they hurt my hands and I can't play, I'm gonna be really pissed."

But the men headed straight for him, ignoring Cade. Adam blocked the first punch, but with three men attacking him, it wasn't long before one connected. The air whooshed from his lungs. Damn, that hurt. He staggered, another punch striking his upper chest, knocking him two steps back. Gasping for breath, he shook his head to clear it, wincing at the echo of pain in his ribs.

Cade waded in and grabbed one attacker, tossing him aside. The man sprang to his feet with a snarl and charged, kicking out at Adam's feet.

"I'll give you my wallet," Adam gasped, barely missing a fall. "Just back the hell up and I'll get it for you."

One of the attackers sneered. "We don't want your money."

"What do you want?" Cade paused before he let rip with a series of punches in one of the attacker's faces. "Aw, damn." He moaned and held his head when a fist clipped him. "That hurt."

Running footsteps sounded behind. Hell! Not good. Three against two wasn't bad. Four against two wouldn't work. Adam dodged a blow and risked a glance into the darkness. Nate!

"Good timing." Adam jerked to the left. He picked a man and started punching, wincing at the thud of fist against flesh. He hoped he didn't make too much of a mess of his hands.

Nate threw himself into the brawl, dispersing one attacker with ease. He approached Adam and a second attacker, determination written on his face.

Three of them evened the odds. The attackers fell back. One scrambled away, fading into the darkness. The other two, outnumbered now, tried to escape.

"Running away?" Adam taunted. Sweet Jesus, his arm ached.

Nate grabbed one of the remaining men and twisted his right arm behind his back. "What do you want?"

"Nothing."

Nate's mouth curled up, his face hard and implacable, a fact Adam noted even in the dim light. "What do you want?" he repeated.

"Someone paid us," the man cried out. "Damn, you're hurtin' me."

"Good." Cade pulled out his cell phone.

"You can't call the sheriff," one of the men protested. "I'll go to jail."

"You should have thought of that first," Nate snarled. "Adam, you okay? Cade?"

"I'm fine," Adam said, lying through his teeth. He'd do the manly thing if it killed him, but the truth was all he wanted to do was crawl into his bed and sleep. His ribs hurt and his cheekbone ached like hell and he thought the gash on his arm from the bullet might have started bleeding again. Lucky the men had missed his mouth, because a fat lip made singing impossible.

Thankfully, someone from the sheriff's department arrived within ten minutes.

"You again," he said when he climbed from the driver's seat.

"Bad day," Adam said. He was acutely aware of the solid heat coming from Nate, who stood behind him. The only thing better than bed at the moment would be if Nate was in there with him, curled behind with his arms wrapped around him. Yeah, Adam could get into that scenario—Nate's lips caressing his neck. That would make him feel better. Much better.

The lawman noted the details of the attack and took the two offenders away.

"What made you change your mind about drinks with

the others?" Cade asked. "Not that I'm complaining. With timing like that, you should play with the band."

"I decided I needed sleep more than I wanted a drink," Nate said.

"Thanks," Adam said. "You saved our asses."

They walked onto the hotel grounds and made their way to Adam and Cade's room, all three coming to an abrupt halt outside. The front door swung ajar.

"You sure you locked the door?" Nate asked.

Adam stared at the door, an awful feeling sinking to the pit of his stomach. Anger took hold, and he shoved the door hard, reaching around the frame to switch on the light.

"Fuck," Cade growled. "If they've stolen or damaged my guitar, there's gonna be hell to pay."

"Wait," Nate said, grabbing a fistful of Cade's shirt before he leapt into the room. "Ring the sheriff again. They might get fingerprints."

Adam stared at his guitar case. It was open, his prized guitar nowhere in sight. His anger morphed into pure fury, his hands fisting at his sides. His eyes narrowed, his entire body tensing while he struggled to maintain control. What the fuck? What the fuck had he done to deserve all the crap chucked at him today?

Two hours later, Cade left to meet his woman and

Adam and Nate collected some clothes. The sheriff had recommended they change accommodations for the night. Cade intended to stay out anyway, and Adam supposed he'd grab a hotel room on his own.

Nate held up a T-shirt and pointed to a pair of jeans. "None of these are fit to wear. Let's go." He grasped Adam's shoulder, gently shunting him toward the door. "I'll lend you something until you can grab some new stuff."

"What about my guitar? My saxophone?" The sense of violation was like a knife in the gut. Sharp. Destructive. Replacing instruments wasn't as easy as replacing clothes.

"I don't know." Nate pushed his shoulder harder and yawned. "We'll work it out tomorrow. We'll check at reception to see if they have a spare room for the rest of the night."

They didn't, since they were full, but they went out of their way to find Adam a room, ringing around, full of apologies for the inconvenience. Finally, they told him they'd located a room at a hotel down the road.

"You shouldn't be alone," Nate said, returning to the office to hear the receptionist tell Adam about the room. "I'll come with you. Would you call a taxi for us, please?" he asked the receptionist.

Suddenly his day was looking up. Adam turned to Nate,

scanning his impassive features. Unfortunately his hat screened most of his face. "You don't have to. I'll be fine on my own."

"This is the third thing today," Nate pointed out while the receptionist rang for the requested cab. "Security is part of my job."

"Is that all I am to you?" Adam asked in a low voice. "A job?"

"Of course not. You're my friend," Nate said.

Not the answer he wanted. Adam's shoulders slumped, Nate's words another kick in the gut. He climbed into the taxi when it arrived, sliding across the backseat so Nate could enter. Adam didn't want that kind of friendship. He wanted a lover, a man who would stay at his side out of love *and* friendship. If Nate intended to stay with him out of obligation, he should think again.

Adam remained silent throughout the short trip to the hotel. He checked in speedily, signing where the receptionist indicated, not really listening as she and Nate exchanged pleasantries.

The room was on the fourth floor. Adam rode the elevator and walked along the thickly carpeted passage to the room at the end. Nate reached past him and slid the keycard into the door. A green light glowed, and Nate pushed the door open.

"You're quiet," Nate said, jerking him from his sulk.

"You don't have to stay. I don't need a nursemaid. What I need is a lover."

"That right?"

"Yeah."

Nate pushed Adam into the room and stepped in after him. He closed the door and slid the security chain across. He slipped the keycard into a slot by the door and flipped another switch. Suddenly the room was bathed in soft light. Adam stared, swallowed. He closed his eyes and opened them again.

"You have got to be kiddin'," he muttered. "The honeymoon suite?"

"It was all they had," Nate said, yanking off his hat and dropping it on a handy coffee table. He removed his footwear and pulled his T-shirt over his head, baring acres of tanned, muscular flesh to Adam. His hands went to his jeans, and he opened the top button.

"What are you doing?" Adam's voice came out low, husky. He ripped his gaze from temptation. Unfortunately his attention went right back to Nate like a heat-guided missile.

Nate slid his jeans down his legs, taking his tight boxers with them. "I'm going to turn on the spa bath the receptionist mentioned and soak for a bit. Ease some of the bruising." Naked, he walked away, leaving Adam staring after him in confusion. This was the same man who'd said he wasn't gay and didn't like men? He shook his head, wincing at the shard of pain. Those men must have hit him harder than he thought.

CHAPTER FOUR

NATE HAD NO IDEA what he was doing. He hadn't seduced another man for years, but after the shooting, the attack and the robbery, he decided he didn't have the luxury to prevaricate. Life was short. Rosa had taught him that, told him to grasp love where he found it and not to pine for her after she died. At the time, he'd told her to shush and not talk that way.

But she'd been right, his conscience whispered. The thought of not having Adam around worried him more than anything else.

A missed opportunity he would mourn.

Nate turned on the taps and water gushed into the tub. He'd liked Adam from their first meeting, and the feeling had grown with time. They'd kissed, held each other. Now

Adam was in danger, and he couldn't walk away without exploring this *thing* between them.

After testing the heat, Nate climbed into the tub and, once the water level was high enough, started the jets churning. Nice. If he had plenty of money, he'd get a large tub like this and put it in the garden, a place where he could soak privately and not worry about clothes. Naked was better. He leaned back and closed his eyes, letting the warm water soak away the ache in his ribs where one of the assailants had landed a punch. No doubt, he'd have a large bruise tomorrow. Nate took comfort from the fact the other guy would look worse.

Something weird was going on in this town, and Adam was in the middle of it.

Nate thought back over the day and frowned. The gunfire this morning hadn't been an accident. His gut instinct shouted that clearly.

A soft splash of water, followed by the brush of a muscled leg against his, told him Adam was joining him. Finally.

"About time you got here," Nate said without opening his eyes. "I need someone to scrub my back."

A long pause. "What did your last slave die of?"

"Insubordination," Nate said with a sly grin.

"I don't like bossy men."

Nate cracked his eyes open a fraction, holding back the smile threatening to bloom. Adam looked like a kid with a pout. Nate waited, not saying anything. He heard a sharp huff of sound, another splash as Adam settled fully into the water.

"Lean forward so I can reach," Adam said, his tone ungracious.

"Better watch it. Your sweet talk might seduce me."

Adam snorted, and Nate allowed his grin to spread. He still had no idea what he was doing where Adam was concerned. This was fun, though. He shifted, angling his body toward Adam, and leaned forward to allow the other man easier access.

"I don't understand you," Adam said finally.

"I'm an uncomplicated kinda guy."

Adam let out a sexy sigh. "Yeah?"

"Yeah."

"You didn't want me to touch you before and now you're practically offering yourself on a plate. I didn't think you were interested. That you weren't gay."

"I'm not gay." Nate frowned inwardly at his quick retort because his words gave the wrong impression. "I like you," he added.

"And that should make me feel special?"

"Hell if I know." It was both that simple and that

complicated. Nate was playing this scenario by ear.

Adam rubbed a soapy washcloth over his shoulders, using hard pressure that made Nate want to groan out loud. Felt good. Real good.

"I'm going to want more than kisses," Adam said, his tone belligerent as if he wanted to argue.

A sense of well-being crept through Nate, the warm water and Adam's attentions making all his residual stress seep away. "Do your worst," Nate said, not inclined to argue. "Although you should probably let me sleep first. I'm an old man compared to you. I need my beauty sleep." Nate turned to glance over his shoulder, fluttering his eyelashes in a flirtatious manner. He earned himself another snort.

Turning away, Nate smiled. At least he'd managed to take Adam's mind off the burglary. Nate knew how attached the men were to their instruments. They were like extensions of their persons. Anyone who touched their treasured guitars committed a sin. A new one always took time to get used to, and he wondered what Adam and Cade would do, since they were playing at the pub the next night.

Not that he intended to bring up the subject now. Adam had enough to worry about without Nate reminding him.

"You're not that much older than me." Adam paused

and tossed aside the washcloth. "Are you going to let me fuck you?"

The harsh words shimmered between them for a long moment. Almost shocking, they held a silent dare.

Nate swallowed, nerves starting a tap dance through his stomach. His cock filled beneath the water, despite his trepidation. His chest heaved in a deep breath. "No, I'm going to fuck you."

"Brave words, but I don't believe you. And I want to know why you've changed your mind."

Damn. Nate hesitated, but he knew there was no way around it. The truth always worked best, even if it hurt or raised matters he'd prefer not to discuss.

"It was something Rosa said to me a long time ago. She told me that after she died she wanted me to keep myself open to finding love again."

"But you haven't," Adam said. "You haven't gone out with anyone in all the time you've worked with the band."

"Are you keeping tabs on me?"

"No, not really. I liked...like you. I was curious and started to pay attention."

"And you decided to approach me because you noticed I didn't go out with women. You figured I was gay?"

"No. No, it was nothing like that. We're on the road a lot, spend time together. It's hard not to notice things."

Nate nodded, knowing Adam spoke the truth. "Is that why you date now and then, ask women out? So the rest of us think you're picky?"

"Yeah. You won't tell, will you?"

"The rest of the band will guess there's something between us," Nate said, ignoring Adam's question. If the man didn't trust him now, there was no hope for them. His brow furrowed as he thought about the situation. It would be difficult not to see they cared for one another. They spent a lot of time together now. The rest of the band probably whispered already.

"Not if we're careful."

"And what if things don't work between us?" Nate hesitated before speaking again. Truth was best, he told himself. Be upfront now. "What happens if we end up hating each other?"

"I hope we're mature enough to work through things without creating problems for everyone else." Adam paused. "Man, do you discuss every relationship to death? What happened to spontaneity?"

Nate shook his head. "Mock all you want. I'm not sure—"

"Were you like this with Rosa?"

Anger pulsed through Nate without warning, hot and consuming. He stood abruptly, water dripping down his body. Ignoring Adam's startled look, Nate stepped from the tub and grabbed a towel. He rubbed it across his chest and the rest of his body with brutal strokes. He strode to the bed and pulled back the sheets. Adam had no right bringing Rosa into their discussion. He didn't know her. Nate switched off all the lights in the bedroom, apart from one of the lamps illuminating the bed. Resolutely, he closed his eyes and prayed for sleep.

A mistake.

With his eyes closed, every other sense magnified. He heard the faint splashing of water, a low hum and a few garbled words coming from the tub. Adam was singing. Nate cursed softly and turned over, hoping to block the sound. Then he heard a louder splash of water, the gurgle as the plug released and the water escaped down the drain. In his mind's eye, he visualized Adam standing in the tub, water streaming down the coffee-colored skin of his chest, the whorls of his tattoo. *Damn, this had to stop.* This was a mistake after all. A relationship with Adam was impossible. It wouldn't take long for the rest of the band to discover something was going on between them. They weren't stupid. And he hated to think what would happen if Stampede's manager found out. Bad publicity. Some people were weird when it came to different. They liked things neat and tidy. All their pegs in the correct holes.

A bark of humor escaped. Damn, this wasn't a laughing matter.

Besides, he wasn't gay. He didn't believe in labels. It was the person who attracted him—their personality. It had nothing to do with male or female.

"I know you're not asleep, Nate."

The cover lifted and he felt Adam crawl into bed with him. Nate opened his mouth to tell Adam to sleep somewhere else, that he'd changed his mind. *Hell*. A bit of honesty here. He wanted Adam in the same bed. He also knew himself well enough to admit to fear. If Adam was in the same bed and made the first move, he could tell himself the man had seduced him. Yup. Screwed-up thinking for sure.

Nate turned over, his breath hitching when he caught Adam's seductive smile. It spread across his face, lighting his brown eyes and making the corners of Nate's mouth twitch with the need to return the smile.

"I'm not going to seduce you. You need to meet me halfway, Nate. I'm not going to give you excuses to trot out later. I want you. I want more than friendship, but I'm not going to force it on you. Anything between us needs to be your decision."

"Fuck!"

"Yes," Adam said in a solemn tone.

Nate wasn't sure which one of them moved first, but their arms wrapped around each other. Their lips touched in a kiss of exploration, tentative even though they'd kissed earlier. Adam cupped Nate's face with one hand, deepening the contact. He nipped on Nate's bottom lip, the sting zapping through Nate's body like the charge of a live wire. A gasp escaped him and Adam took advantage, sliding his tongue into Nate's mouth. Nate didn't even try to pull away, admitting he needed this. The close contact of a person he liked and cared for. The clean scent of soap rose from Adam's skin. It smelled better than the reeking perfume from the other night.

Kissing a man wasn't that different when it came down to it. Adam's lips were just as soft, and Nate found the contrast of his stubble appealing, memories of long-ago explorations before Rosa drifting back to him.

Adam groaned and moved closer until their bodies touched from shoulder to groin. He dragged Nate against his chest, and a frisson of pleasure darted the length of Nate's body. Pushing thoughts of right or wrong aside, Nate went with the sensations, the roughness of Adam's cheek when he cupped it with his hand, the hardness of his chest and the silky smoothness and lazy stroke of his tongue as they kissed. Adam's mouth was hot, his lips demanding while his hands stroked across Nate's back and lower to cup his ass. Blood pooled at Nate's groin, the purpose and skill of Adam's touch making him shiver. Needy. Desperate for more. Nate pulled away, breathing hard.

"Let me make you feel good," Adam said. "We'll take it slow. No sex tonight. Just touching. Learning each other." As he spoke, his hands wandered, overburdening Nate's nerve endings with electric sensation.

Nate stared at Adam, noted the heavy-lidded look and knew he probably looked equally aroused. His cock certainly was, hard and aching with the sweet agony of anticipation.

"Nate?"

"Yeah?" His voice emerged in a guttural tone, holding all the need pulsing inside his body. "Please touch me," he added, knowing he needed to give Adam more reassurance before the other man would touch him more aggressively. He shifted against Adam and couldn't hold back his groan of pleasure when the head of his cock slid across Adam's hip.

Adam flashed him a grin before laying a trail of kisses down his jaw and neck. He nipped lightly at the junction of shoulder and neck, making Nate wince. The lap of Adam's tongue soothed the sting and sent all kinds of messages streaming through his body. A hungry noise squeezed past his tight lips. Adam lifted his head, his warm breath caressing Nate's face. Nate swallowed, his mouth suddenly dry, his heart hammering against his ribs in an erratic manner.

"Just touching," Adam reminded him, stroking his fingers across Nate's chest, mapping his pectoral muscles. "Nothing to worry about." He moved his lower body so their legs tangled and their groins brushed.

Nate froze when their cocks slid against each other, the instant pleasure an erotic assault on his last reservations. Being with Adam felt damn good, and he wanted to be with his friend.

His eyes fluttered closed to focus on the pleasure. He felt a stream of warm air ripple across his nipple, felt his cock buck. Then Adam sucked on his nipple, the sharp suction edging toward painful.

"Damn," Nate muttered. His cock throbbed while pinpricks of pleasure flowed through him.

"Feel good?"

Yeah. Way better than it should. Nate kept his mouth shut, worried about articulating exactly how he felt. Hell, he wasn't sure he could.

"So good you're not talkin', huh?" Adam chuckled and ran his hand down Nate's body, across his ribs and over his hip. It was as if fire followed his touch. Nate groaned, but things became even better when Adam grasped his cock in a firm grip. No tentative handling. This was a man who knew what he was doing.

Adam shifted closer and released Nate's cock. Nate's eyes flicked open and captured Adam's gaze. Adam's eyes sparkled with life and a hint of challenge, halting the instinctive protest tickling the tip of Nate's tongue. Nate firmed his mouth and held his protest. Go with the flow. He wanted this. At least his heart did. The struggle in his mind was another thing.

"You'll like this," Adam promised, seconds before he gripped Nate's cock along with his own. He pumped his hand up and down, his grip tight to a point shy of pain.

"Damn, that feels good." Nate hissed at the combination of pain and pleasure, the ache in his balls growing rapidly.

"I should have used lube," Adam said. "Put it down to impatience. It'll feel even better once our cocks get slippery. Yeah. See? Like that," Adam said, letting their shafts rub together while working his callused hand over the sensitive heads.

"Better? It'll get better than this?" Nate jerked off when he was on his own, when he needed release, but this...this was ten times better. The memories of the last time with a man were a dim memory. Something he hadn't thought of for years. Yeah, being with Adam this way made him feel great. Another stroke caused his balls to draw exquisitely tight, and he didn't even think about holding back.

He gripped Adam's shoulders and sought his lips, kissing the man and shoving every lingering doubt away. Their mouths moved together while Adam kept pumping their cocks in his fist. The kiss deepened, tongues flirted, and soft, needy sounds built up in Nate's chest. Until now, he hadn't realized how much he'd missed the intimacy of being with another human, giving and receiving pleasure. Oh, he'd thought about it, but being with Adam drove the fact home. He'd been starving for the touch of a lover.

Adam pulled back, separating their mouths. "You have to hang around and see if I can make good on my promise that it gets better." His fist caught the delicate underside of Nate's cock. With an easy glide of his fingers, Adam repeated the move.

Nate studied him through the heavy fog of desire. His cock swelled even harder. Then, with the strength of a sucker punch, his orgasm ripped through him, semen spurting against their chests.

"Perfect," Adam said, his voice velvet-rough. He closed his eyes, and Nate watched him, saw the tension, the moment he couldn't hold back an instant longer. His hand stilled and climax took him. His mouth opened in a soundless groan, the chords in his neck straining as his come splashed their bodies.

Gradually, he stilled, and his mouth curled in a sexy smile. "Damn, I want to do that again. I want to do everything with you." Before Nate had a chance to reply, he jumped off the bed and strode into the bathroom.

Nate heard the rush of water when Adam turned on the taps and, minutes later, he returned with a damp washcloth. Nate sat up, grimacing at the stickiness on his chest and belly.

Adam's jaw cracked open in a wide yawn. "Man, I'm tired." When Nate went to take the washcloth from him, he batted his hands away. "Let me. Any excuse to touch you." With competent strokes, he cleaned up and tossed the cloth on the floor beside the bed. He switched off the light and climbed back into the king-size bed.

Relaxed and replete, Nate let Adam drape himself around him. Sighing softly, Nate closed his eyes and let sleep take him. He'd worry about any problems gunning for them tomorrow.

※※※※※※ ※※※※※※

THEY'D FAILED. *AGAIN*. ADAM was alive and well, still a threat to him. Damn, his brother had more luck than an

Irishman holding a bouquet of four-leaf clovers.

You reap what you sow.

Those had been the bitter words uttered by a village woman when he'd charged her to sleep with him. Desperate for a baby, she'd paid. They all paid, and he couldn't see what was wrong with the new rules he'd instigated. It wasn't as if Adam would have slept with them, ensuring a fruitful harvest and children to inherit. No, he would have merely touched them and offered the traditional blessing.

They didn't understand. He had expenses. Staff to pay. A home to run. Singlehandedly he'd taken the legend of Kokopelli into the future, made his calling into a full-time job. The people didn't comprehend the need for change, but he did. Stagnant ways brought low growth, and prosperity suffered.

Thanks to him, the people had food, despite the droughts and the low rate of fertility. The money he generated kept them all alive, yet none of them appreciated it.

Justin thumped his hands against the steering wheel of the luxury SUV. Summoned home like a servant, even though he'd told the elders he wanted a few weeks off. Kokopelli served the people, they said. He didn't take vacations.

But soon he'd take an enforced one if he wasn't successful in taking his baby brother out of the equation. Justin scowled, not liking the thought or the personal consequences if the elders replaced him as they wanted. They'd even ignore Adam's homosexuality, the reason they'd replaced him in the first place.

What should he do now?

He couldn't afford to have another misstep, which meant there was only one option available to him. He'd have to back off for a few weeks. The elders didn't know Adam's location because they hadn't been smart enough to keep tabs on him. Yeah, he'd back off and meantime pay someone to watch Adam. Maybe he could recruit someone in the band or the road crew to report on Adam's activities. He'd have to use guile, because otherwise the band would become suspicious. A reporter perhaps? Would they consider letting a reporter travel with the band?

Not a bad idea, but this time he'd sleep on it for a few days before he acted.

Nodding decisively, Justin indicated a right turn and drove down the dusty track leading to the village. After driving through the village, he turned left, the tarmac under the wheels less bone jarring than the bumpy dirt track. He pulled up outside a sprawling hacienda with relief. Home.

Justin climbed from the SUV and stalked up the three steps leading to the large decorative wooden door. It opened seconds before he reached it.

A dusky-skinned woman wearing a black gown greeted him with a smile. "Good evening, Mr. James. How was the conference?"

Justin ran his gaze over her curves, showcased to perfection in the figure-skimming gown. "Lara, it went well. The topics of discussion were most enlightening. And you, my dear. How are you?" He stepped inside, closed the door and took her in his arms, placing a quick kiss on her upturned lips.

She moaned softly, pressing closer and clinging.

At her invitation, Justin deepened the kiss and lifted her into his arms. He strode along the passage leading to his bedroom, smiling in approval when he saw the bed turned back and the muted glow from the bedside lamps.

After toeing off his black dress shoes, he placed Lara on the bed.

The room smelled of lemons and the floral sweetness of Lara's perfume. Soon, it would smell of musky sex and arousal. His cock tightened at the thought. Ironic, really. Lara was one of many women who tended to his needs. A favorite. All of this would be wasted on Adam. No doubt if he returned, he'd stick to the old ways and send the village back two hundred years in time.

The elders would push Justin to the background, discarding him like yesterday's trash. Justin shrugged off his jacket, his gaze running across the smooth skin of Lara's bare shoulders to the ample curves barely concealed beneath the bodice of her gown.

No, he refused to give up this lifestyle, which meant his brother had to go. He'd go with the reporter idea and keep contact with things that way. Let the dust settle and their wariness disperse, then he'd strike.

And maybe it was time to think about having a son to secure the succession. Yes, he thought, suddenly exhilarated about the idea of a dynasty. It was all within his grasp if he played the correct cards.

Adam was the only one who stood in his way.

CHAPTER FIVE

ADAM WOKE TO A hard cock pressed against his backside. For the instant it took to orient himself, confusion reigned, then he remembered. *Nate*. A smile spread across his lips as he slowly turned over. Still asleep, Nate looked younger, the stern expression relaxed for once and not obscured by his trademark Stetson.

Adam took the opportunity to ogle the other man, taking in his broad chest and muscles dusted with dark hair. The light beard, usually well groomed, looked darker than normal and covered his entire jaw because Nate hadn't trimmed away the stubble for a couple of days. An equally light moustache framed his sensual lips, lips the man knew how to use to advantage. Adam's cock bucked and his smile widened as he recalled the sensation of Nate's mouth moving against his. Yeah, the man knew how to kiss, which made Adam wonder how those lips would feel wrapped around his cock. Something for the near future. A frown replaced the smile. He hoped, as long as Nate didn't freak on him and backtrack.

Nothing about this seduction was easy, which was probably why Adam was enjoying himself so much. There was a danger of getting hurt. He knew it, accepted the risk because he'd known Nate for a while, and sometimes a man had to take a leap of faith. Once Nate made a decision, he stuck to it. But he knew this decision was a huge one for Nate, and the other man wasn't one hundred percent sure of a relationship with him. It was difficult fighting the ghost of a dead wife. The good memories.

Adam continued his perusal, his gaze tracing the way the dark hair on his chest thinned to arrow down toward Nate's groin. One of Nate's many good bits. Nate was a big man, his cock in perfect proportion, and this morning standing to attention.

Temptation nipped at Adam. Another quick glance reassured him Nate still slept. Moving cautiously, Adam inched down the bed until he was level with Nate's groin. Unable to resist, he stroked his hand over Nate's hip, noting the paler skin normally hidden by his clothes. Nate stirred, but didn't wake, and Adam took his time exploring. He ran his tongue over Nate's hip and down to the crease where leg met groin. Adam savored the faint saltiness of Nate's skin, the heat coming off his body. He couldn't believe Nate was actually here, in bed with him. It was something he'd wanted for a long time, and now that he had him here...

Adam smirked and moved in on Nate's cock. He ran a light finger down Nate's dick from base to tip before wrapping his hand around the shaft. The contrast of hard and soft met his approval. Then the need to taste this intimate part of Nate rippled through him and, with another glance at Nate's face, he lowered his head. Dragging his tongue across the head of Nate's cock, Adam tasted him for the first time. A groan whispered past his lips, and Adam settled in to explore, learning his size and shape, the way he tasted.

Nate's cock hardened further under his ministrations, and Adam glanced up without removing his mouth. Watching Nate's face closely, he alternatively sucked and laved, swirling his tongue across the tiny slit on top.

One moment Nate was asleep and the next, his entire body stiffened. "Adam?" The gritty morning voice curled through Adam. Arousal grabbed his cock, lengthening it. Damn, he hoped Nate wouldn't make him stop. He needed this—a connection.

Nate's hands came down to grip his shoulders, and Adam lifted his head, his mouth quirking when he noticed the tinge of arousal glittering in Nate's eyes. At least it wasn't shock. Nate hadn't leapt from the bed, cursing him. Yet.

"Are you okay with this?" Adam didn't want to give Nate the chance to deny his participation at a later date. And it could happen. The man was skittish.

Nate's Adam's apple bobbed as he swallowed. His eyes closed for an instant, and Adam's heart sank. He was going to tell him to stop.

"Yeah. Yeah, I'm okay."

It took a second for Nate's reply to sink in. When it registered, Adam grinned with pleasure. Continuing to watch Nate's face, he pumped Nate's cock slowly. Once. Twice, before he took him in his mouth again and applied suction, allowing the flat of his tongue to drag across the underside of Nate's cock.

The swift intake of air and the stark tension on Nate's face gave him hope. When he dragged his tongue across the head again, Nate's hips bucked upward, pushing his cock deeper into Adam's mouth. Going with instinct, Adam did to Nate everything he enjoyed a lover doing to him, salty beads of pre-come his reward.

"Damn," Nate said, his words not much more than a

groan. A tremor shook his large frame, and his hands came down to cradle Adam's head. "I thought I was dreaming."

Nate dreamed about him. The knowledge made his stomach flip, a combination of pleasure and relief settling on him. Maybe the fight to win the man wouldn't turn into a battle. Adam wasn't sure how he felt about that when he'd prepared for a war. He reached up to tweak one of Nate's nipples. The guttural moan made him smile. Damn, he liked this man. Wanted him desperately. He was willing to fight for him, yet a part of him felt cheated at Nate's surrender, which begged the question: Was he playing games with Nate? Adam sucked on Nate's dick again and immediately rejected the thought. Nah. He really liked Nate. They were friends. Friends and now lovers. A good combination. Yeah, he could imagine being with Nate for a long time, and for a man who had taken things one day at a time since he was a teenager, this was huge. Nothing about the realization frightened him, which told him he was right to pursue Nate.

Wanting to talk, Adam dragged his mouth off Nate's cock, slowly, to maximize the sensations for his lover. Okay, so he wanted to torture Nate a little for taking so long to come around to his way of thinking.

"Was it a good dream or a bad one?" They needed honesty between them. If they didn't have truth, they had nothing. Without warning, Adam's past intruded. He thought of his family, the family who had rejected him because he preferred men to women. The family who still rejected him.

Ashamed and mortified by his preferences, they'd told him to leave and never return.

During the years since, he'd wandered, searched for unconditional love. Still searching. Always searching.

Adam frowned, staring at Nate, wanting a clue as to the man's feelings and thoughts. Normally able to read people well, when it came to Nate he didn't have a clue.

"You gonna stare at me all day or get me off?" Nate asked in a husky voice.

"You're confusing," Adam blurted. "Sometimes you behave like a virgin teen, all wide-eyed and shocked, and at other times you're blunt and to the point." He shook his head. "I never know how you're gonna react." Nate kept him off-balance. A challenge. Maybe it was all about the thrill of the chase. Who the hell knew? Bottom line, Nate baffled him.

Nate snorted. "You don't want an easy man. You'd get bored."

"I don't get bored."

Nate's dark brows rose. "No?"

"No. I thought you'd panic if you woke up to me

sucking your cock," he confessed, not liking the direction of the conversation. Adam decided talking wasn't a great idea after all. Too much discussion might cause problems. Nate might decide to leave the bed, for one.

"I like morning sex."

Adam scowled in earnest. "A man could feel used hearing comments like that." He gestured at his cock, rearing from his groin in distinct interest. "Are you going to return the favor?"

Nate tensed, averting his gaze. Yeah, exactly what he'd thought. Nate was acting like the outraged virgin again, and later he'd accuse Adam of seducing him.

"I don't know." Nate surprised him by actually answering. He turned back to capture Adam's gaze. "You make me feel good, but I keep thinking about Rosa."

Rosa again. Adam started to slide away, but Nate made a sound. He moved fast, slapping a hand on Adam's shoulder to hold him in place. "No, don't stop."

Their gazes met, held.

The air hissed from Adam's lungs.

"Aw, what the hell." Giving up, Adam lowered his head and went for the kill, using every bit of his expertise to make Nate come. He covered the tip of Nate's cock with his mouth and moved down, gradually taking him deeper. Unable to watch Nate any longer, he closed his eyes, concentrating instead on his other senses. He tasted the salty liquid leaking from the tip each time it spilled on his tongue, heard the soft groan of pleasure from Nate and felt Nate's hands burrow into his hair.

Nate's hands tightened, gripping his head almost painfully. If he'd had longer hair, his eyes would have teared with the sting. The jerk of pain flashed through Adam's body and filled his cock with blood.

He caressed Nate's balls and lower shaft with his hands while his mouth and tongue pushed his lover higher. Nate groaned, letting Adam touch him without reservation. Adam smiled around Nate's cock and decided to push him harder. He ran one of his fingers up Nate's shaft toward the head, opening his mouth so his finger slipped inside. Once he was sure his finger was nice and wet, he removed it, intending to push Nate even more. While he kept up the suction on Nate's cock, he moved his damp finger down until it skimmed across Nate's hole.

Nate tensed, a garbled sound of protest coming from him before Adam distracted him with his mouth and tongue, taking him deep into his throat and swallowing around the head of Nate's cock. While he did this, he played with Nate's puckered entrance.

"Fuck," Nate muttered, his hips jerking upward.

Adam grasped the opportunity and played with more

aggression. Soon Nate twisted and squirmed and didn't protest when Adam stroked his finger inside.

Nate swore again and shivered, climaxing suddenly.

Yes! He wanted to shout in elation, but he was too busy swallowing. Gradually, Nate's dick softened and, with a final stroke of his tongue, Adam lifted his head. He removed his finger from Nate's ass.

They stared at each other. Nate was the first to look away. Adam waited for him to say something. He didn't.

What the hell had he expected? A bloody medal? Sighing, Adam climbed off the bed and stalked to the en suite without another word. He started the shower and stepped inside, closing the glass doors after him. The shower was large enough for three adults, with several showerheads, designed to massage and offer all sorts of sensual delights. Wasted today.

He grabbed a handful of the shower gel from the special dispenser and scrubbed it over his chest and under his arms. Closing his eyes, he let the water pour over him. The squeak of the shower door snapped his eyes open.

Nate stepped into the cubicle, closing the door after him. "Why did you run off?"

"I didn't think there was anything to say."

Nate reached for the shower gel and squirted some into his palm. "You took me by surprise. I wasn't expecting to wake up that way."

Adam shrugged. He thought they'd talked about that, settled it already. A man could take only so much rejection before he walked. The way Nate ran hot and cold didn't bode well for the happily-ever-after dreams he'd been busy conjuring.

Nate grabbed a washcloth and lathered it up. "I didn't think you'd sulk."

Stung, Adam muttered, "I don't sulk." He glared at Nate, his right hand clenched at his side.

"Then finish your shower and come back to bed," Nate said. "It's still early. We don't need to be anywhere until this afternoon."

A spurt of anger made Adam testy. "Don't do me any favors." He scrubbed his groin, ignoring his hard-on and the hungry burst of pleasure. He would not jerk off with Nate watching.

Nate grasped one shoulder and jerked Adam around to face him. "I'm not. I want this."

"What about Rosa? Is she going to come between us all the time?" Damn, now he sounded jealous.

"Rosa is dead. I'm not." Nate sighed. "Look, Rosa was a large part of my life. I miss her. I'm going to think about her sometimes. But I have feelings for you and I want to explore them." His brown eyes burned with intensity. "If that's what you want."

Another silent stare as they measured and weighed each other's responses.

"Okay?"

Adam relaxed a fraction. "Okay." Hell, he hoped Nate wasn't stringing him along. He didn't think he could bear that.

Nate smiled and closed the distance between them until their chests touched. Lowering his head, he snatched a kiss, laughing when their noses collided. Finally, they managed to get it right, and the teasing kiss turned serious. Their lower bodies brushed, cocks rubbing together. Need simmered through Adam. Longing. He wanted to grip Nate's hips and thrust into him, using hard, no-nonsense strokes until they both shuddered with the power of their desire. Yeah, that was what he wanted.

Wasn't gonna happen. Not yet.

Adam was afraid if he pushed Nate too hard, he'd run again, despite his brave words of wanting more between them. Of course, there were alternatives.

Adam pulled away. "You ready to get out yet?"

Nate reached for the gel. "Give me a bit longer." He washed and rinsed off the soap while Adam pushed open the door and stepped out of the shower. Grabbing a towel, he dried off rapidly before wrapping the damp towel around his waist and heading for the phone.

By the time Nate came out, he'd ordered breakfast and coffee and pulled on a pair of jeans.

"I thought I'd find you in bed," Nate said.

"I ordered coffee." Adam's breath caught. Nate was eyeing his chest in a distinctly predatory manner.

Nate's eyes narrowed. "Good idea." He opened his mouth to say something else and stopped when someone knocked on the door. "Better go and put on some clothes."

"Don't dress on my account." Adam grabbed some money from his wallet for a tip and went to answer the summons.

"Check to see who it is first," Nate warned, pausing on his way to the bedroom. "Make sure they're wearing the same uniform as the guys last night." He disappeared, returning seconds later, buttoning his jeans as he strode barefoot across the luxurious carpet.

Adam snorted, but squinted through the peephole anyway. "It's someone on the staff," he said, opening the door.

"This time." Nate sauntered over to the curtains and pulled them back, letting in the early morning light. "It might not be every time. Caution won't hurt. Too many strange things happened yesterday."

The young woman picked up the breakfast tray off her

cart and carried it into their room, setting it on top of a small wooden table.

"Thanks," Adam said, handing over a tip.

She thanked him and left.

"Nothing sinister about her," Adam said.

"Smug doesn't become you."

Adam grinned, liking that Nate didn't treat him like royalty. Some of the management team did because he was the lead singer, the rising star. If Nate thought he was talking shit, Nate told him. It had always been that way. "Want some coffee?"

"Yeah."

Adam poured two cups and handed over a black to Nate, doctoring his own with cream and a packet of sugar.

Nate stared at him over his steaming coffee cup. "I thought it was your hard-on making you testy, and all the time it was lack of caffeine."

"Why are you pushing?" Adam demanded. "Is it so I'll take charge and you won't have to think? Because if it is, you should reconsider. I'm not doing anything to you or with you without your approval. No way am I gonna give you the opportunity to cry foul at a later date."

Nate sipped his coffee. "Damn, you're no fun."

"I'm serious."

"I know. It's true I'm having a few problems readjusting

my thinking. It's been Rosa for me for a long time, ya know?"

Adam nodded, although he couldn't stop his leap of resentment toward the woman. He strove to hide it and thought he managed okay because Nate's expression didn't alter. Adam took a deep breath and shoved Rosa to the back of his mind. He didn't need to think about her. "I envy you having a constant partner. I haven't had any serious relationships."

"Why?" Nate settled on a chair by the window and stretched out his legs.

Adam watched the flex of Nate's chest, admired the play of muscles beneath the denim of his jeans. He stared into his coffee cup when what he really wanted to do was close the distance between them and run his hands over Nate's sexy body.

"Adam?"

How much should he tell Nate? Stick close to the truth. That might work best. "I lived in a small town and didn't get out much. I had commitments at home."

"What sort of commitments?"

Adam didn't think Nate was ready to learn about his family history. He'd tell him later, if it looked as if they really had a future. That would be time enough to tell him tales about Kokopelli and his family bloodlines. "My father wasn't well. They needed me to help out on the ranch."

"How come I never knew you came from a ranching background?"

"Because I live and breathe music," Adam said with a chuckle. "We've always talked about songwriting and bands and the next gig on the horizon. Farming isn't my thing."

"What about your father?"

The humor fell away. "He disowned me. Didn't want a queer son. It didn't matter to him if I was in the closet or not. He didn't appreciate skeletons in *his* family closet. We argued. I left."

"That's rough," Nate said, his brown eyes saying more, holding sympathy. Understanding. "It's hard to believe you haven't had a serious relationship."

Hell, he hadn't wanted anyone else once he'd seen Nate. "I haven't had a chance. We're on the road for months at a time. There isn't the opportunity for more than a casual hookup. I'm fine with that." Or at least he used to be okay with that. Now he wanted Nate.

"So, this is casual for you?" Nate's eyes held a hint of vulnerability and hurt. Adam hurried to reassure him.

"Now I've met someone I could get serious about," Adam said, going with honesty. "If he has the guts enough to go for it." Yeah, that was the truth. The words felt right, made him feel confident about the future. He really was in this for the long haul.

"Are you calling me a coward?"

"If the hat fits."

Nate exhaled, the sharp sound hanging in the air between them. "Since Rosa, I haven't looked at another woman. You know that."

"And men?"

"Adam, hell." He dragged an agitated hand through his hair. "Before Rosa, I had a few casual relationships, but once I met her, that was it." He glanced at Adam. "I have slept with a couple of men. Experimented."

"Yeah? You never said. So, you're not a virgin?"

"No, and you never asked. You were too busy trying to seduce me. Are we going to eat or not?"

A change of subject. Adam hid a smirk. Nate never talked much about himself. They were alike in that respect. Turning away, he grabbed the covers off the food, then handed a plate of bacon and scrambled eggs to Nate.

"Cade and I need to sort out replacement guitars this morning, and I'll have to buy another sax."

Nate frowned. "Damn, I'd forgotten about that."

"Good to know the thought of sex with me drives everything from your head."

Nate ignored Adam's comment and reached for his cell phone. "I'll ring Cade now."

"He'll be pissed," Adam said. "You know he hates waking early."

"He's gonna be pissed anyway," Nate said. "Finding new instruments won't be easy."

All true. He'd had his guitar and sax for a long time. They were like old friends and almost an extension of him. Playing another one just wasn't the same. Anger built in Adam, his hands clenching around his knife and fork. The culprit should start running, because if he managed to grab them, their life wouldn't be worth living. "Morgan has a spare. That will take care of one of us. The pub owner is a keen musician. He might know where we can get our hands on replacements." Adam forced himself to start eating his breakfast. He listened to Nate organize Cade to meet them at the hotel. Next he rang the owner of the pub.

"All sorted apart from the sax," Nate said. "The pub owner has guitars you can borrow. They might have a lead on a sax as well. We'll know in a couple of hours."

Adam smiled in bemusement. "I could have done that. I don't need you to take care of me."

The color bleached from Nate's face. He set the cell down on the coffee table with a firm click and stood abruptly, heading for the en suite.

"Wait. Dammit, Nate."

Nate didn't look back. The door shut in a demand for privacy, and Adam sank back onto the couch. Damn, it was two steps forward, one step back with Nate. He didn't know where he was with the other man, and it killed him.

JUSTIN'S BEDROOM DOOR OPENED, and Lara let out a shriek of horror. Justin whipped the covers over her head, tugging her trembling body close to his side while he tamped down his anger. The heavy curtains jerked back, the bright morning sunlight highlighting his father's grizzled appearance and determined face.

"Justin, the petitioners have arrived for the day."

"I was busy," Justin said in a mild voice, fighting an inward struggle for calm. He made sure the covers hid his chest from his father's view. The last thing he needed was for his father to notice the absence of the Kokopelli tattoo. That would cause problems. Lara hadn't mentioned the subject, and he didn't like to bring it up with her and highlight his predicament. Part of the reason for his favoritism in regard to her was the fact she didn't disclose anything of a private nature to others—not as far as he had noticed. His father wouldn't be quite as reticent. Justin met his father's gaze and waited.

"Send the slut home. You sully the Kokopelli name." Distaste dripped from each word. "No wonder crops are declining and people drift from the old ways with the example you give them."

An old argument and one Justin tired of. "I will be ready in half an hour."

Their gazes clashed, and for once Justin didn't back down from his father's will. A look of surprise, followed swiftly by a clipped nod, brought relief to Justin. His father crossed the lavish room with rapid steps, exiting without another word. Justin glanced at his watch, knowing the clock ticked. His father would expect his presence in the conference room in exactly half an hour. If he didn't arrive, his father would come looking for him. Again.

Justin climbed from the king-size bed, grimacing at his erection. "You'd better go, sweetheart," he said. "And stay out of my father's way, hmmm?"

"He called me a slut."

"I know. He's upset with me and taking it out on you. I'm sorry." The one good thing to come from this was meeting Lara. Although he slept with others, Lara was his preferred lover. She understood him, never pressured for a commitment where other women might have taken advantage of the situation. "Are you helping with the petitioners today?"

Lara smoothed her hair. "Yes."

"Good. I'll see you later."

Justin headed for the shower and, half an hour later, strode into the conference room where he met with the petitioners. A sense of peace came over him, as it always did when he walked into this room and pulled on the Kokopelli mantle.

His father had had his time as the caretaker of Kokopelli magic and freely passed the gift to Adam. After their bitter argument, they'd forcibly removed the power from Adam and his younger brother had left. Now his father and the other elders considered Justin unworthy. He refused to go down without a fight.

Despite the flash of anger at his father, Justin forced his mouth into a gentle smile and glanced along the line of waiting women. Young and old, they all wanted one thing. They wanted Justin to give the gift of fertility to their family, to bring fruitful crops and riches. Each day the lines were longer, the pressure to perform greater.

And something was making the magic falter.

Forcing aside his anxiety, Justin went to the start of the line and spoke with the first woman.

"How can I help you?" he asked, already knowing what

she required. Past her childbearing years, she most likely required help with her failing crops. As if the current drought was his fault!

"If this crop fails, the bank will foreclose on our farm. It has been in my family for four generations," she whispered.

Justin held out his left hand, the one bearing the ceremonial Kokopelli ring. Smiling through tear-filmed eyes, she clasped his hand in hers so tightly he feared for his circulation. "Good fortune to you," he replied, waiting while she collected herself and kissed his ring.

The pattern repeated for the next two hours with Justin murmuring the same words over and over until he felt like a robot. With the doors constantly opening and closing, the temperature rose inside the conference room, the air conditioning system laboring to maintain the setting on the dial.

"One moment, please," Justin said to the next person in line, a beautiful teenager with a sultry smile that probably gave her parents nightmares. He stepped aside, speaking to Lara in an undertone. "No more. Tell Pedro to cut off the line and send the rest home."

"Yes, Justin." Lara bustled away, her sensuous form covered with a shapeless robe. The fabric whispered as she departed and, sighing, Justin turned back to the waiting teenager. He wished he could work out a way to delegate, but unfortunately, contact with the people was one of the mainstays of the Kokopelli tradition.

"How can I help you?" Justin asked the teenager.

"I don't wish to have a child," she said. "I'm too young. I want to enjoy myself before I tie myself to one man and become fat with a baby."

Justin jerked with shock. He suspected his mouth dropped open a fraction before he regained control. The girl's dark brown eyes dared him to disagree, attitude spilling from every line of her curvy body. She really expected him to condone this when Kokopelli spread fertility?

"Kokopelli brings fertility," Justin reminded her, fighting the masculine urge to let his gaze wander her tits. The last thing he needed was to give her more ammunition.

"He's not doing such a great job lately," she retorted, thrusting back her shoulders, her firm breasts moving another inch closer to his chest. "The crops have failed again because of the drought, and birth rates have decreased. The women around here are barren." She tossed her head, setting her glossy black curls in motion.

"Then I don't understand why you're petitioning me," Justin said.

"I figure it's something you're doing. You have the

power to make people and crops fruitful, and it stands to reason you have the ability to do the opposite. My observations say you're using your powers to amass wealth. Naughty, *naughty*." She waggled her finger in a chiding motion, her lips pursed in a sexy pout.

Justin knew his mouth dropped open this time. What the hell should he say to that? The sly grin made her look like a contented cat. It jerked him back to his senses. "I suggest if you don't wish to conceive, you abstain from sexual contact. That is the correct way."

She scowled, her eyes flashing with the beginnings of a temper tantrum. "If I wanted a lecture, I would speak with my parents."

"I can't help you." Justin moved back two steps.

"You don't want to help me." Her voice rose with each successive word.

Justin noted the interest and speculation on the part of the other petitioners. "Next, please."

"He won't help me. Kokopelli won't help me." The girl's face held challenge.

The minx knew exactly how to play the scene. And she accused him of blackmail. He couldn't buckle. He'd lose face, and people would start to talk even more than they were now. There were times lately when he found himself envying Adam. At least his brother lived life as he chose—even if he was a queer.

Banking his anger, Justin took her right hand, clasping it between his. "Good fortune to you," he said, uttering the traditional Kokopelli words.

She gasped, her face paling before her chin jerked up in determination. She yanked her hand from his grip. "Don't worry. I'll make sure I pay on the way out." Pure feminine sarcasm laced her tone.

Uneasily, Justin watched her stalk across the floor, the other petitioners parting like the Red Sea. Despite her temper, her hips rolled in a feminine sway. Pure sex on two legs. The boys or men she set her sights on wouldn't stand a chance.

Justin worked his way through the rest of the petitioners, wondering why he cared. The elders wanted to replace him with his younger brother, pushing him aside like unwanted garbage and discounting everything he'd done during the past years. He'd worked hard, dammit. He deserved the kudos that came with the Kokopelli office since he'd devoted his life to the job.

He went through a mental checklist of what he needed to do to maintain the status quo. The reporter idea might work, but that would mean someone else who could cause problems for him in the future. He rejected his earlier idea. Unmarried, he couldn't produce a child of his own, someone to inherit the magic, or at least not in a hurry. The only alternative was to make Adam disappear. He couldn't take the chance that Adam would actually agree to return. Although he'd heard the harsh words spoken between his father and brother, he knew his father wanted to reconcile with his youngest son. Older now, their father had mellowed.

What he forgot was that Justin had held the office, stepped in to help because it was his destiny too. They considered him a replacement. He was tired of the way they treated him as second best.

"Justin, that was the last one," Lara said.

"Thank you." He wiped the beads of sweat off his forehead with his white handkerchief. "It's been a trying day."

"Let me serve you," Lara said. "I will give you a massage."

A wave of love for the woman who had stood at his side engulfed him. Despite the lack of marriage, she believed in him. "I want you to order a special dinner from the chef," Justin said, skimming his fingers across her jaw. "Tell him we'll dine at eight."

"Is it a special occasion?"

It was time. Justin felt it in his gut, and knew this was the right thing to do. It would be a time of celebration amongst the people. They would rejoice, and he would start working on that heir. "Yes, Lara, it is a special occasion. You will dine with me. Wear something nice," he said. "I'll see you this evening. I have several things to take care of this afternoon." Smiling at her, he pressed a swift kiss to her lips and strode from the conference room, through the sumptuous rooms with their paintings and valuable rugs most collectors would hang on their walls, until he reached the privacy of his office. He hurried inside and locked the door, before sitting behind the immense wooden desk and reaching for his phone.

Justin pulled a slip of paper from his wallet and dialed the number written on it. The phone rang for a long time, interrupted by several clicks as it rerouted through the telephone system.

"Wyatt," a metallic voice droned.

Justin's hand trembled, and he swallowed, but his voice sounded firm when he read the seven-digit number off the paper.

"Repeat," the voice demanded.

Justin repeated the number and hung up without speaking another word. The hit was in motion. This time Adam would die because he'd hired a professional with a hundred percent success rate. A tear streaked down his face and regret ached in his throat as he wished, for an instant, that things could have been different.

CHAPTER SIX

NATE WATCHED THE SHOW from the background, the music, the appreciative shouts and singing of the crowd pulsing around him in bursts of excitement. An electric atmosphere ruled tonight, and he felt himself drawn along for the ride. Part of it was Adam, of course. The rest was the music. It was magical. There was no other word for it.

The current song drifted to a close, the last note fading. A cheer rang out. A pair of white lace panties flew through the air to join the others littering the stage like a field of flowers. Applause filled the pub. People sprang to their feet, whistling and stomping in appreciation.

Adam grinned, a flash of white teeth and sparkling eyes, and Nate caught his breath on seeing him. He was beautiful, although Adam would argue if Nate ever told him to his face. Nate smirked. He'd accept sexy. His humor faded as he thought about Adam's kisses and the way they'd touched each other. Uneasy with the burst of pleasure, he shoved the thought away to pull out later. Adam held the audience in the palm of his hand, ruling them with his extraordinary talent. A scowl formed as Nate tried to make sense of the way he felt when he spent time with Adam.

An oath slipped past his lips.

On the small stage, Adam held up his hand, and the crowd, taking his cue, grew silent.

"Last night, someone broke into the hotel where the band is staying," Adam said. "They stole Cade's guitar. They stole mine and they also stole the sax I've had for the last ten years." He turned away to pick up the saxophone Nate knew he'd borrowed from the pub owner's young daughter. "I borrowed this one from a girl called Maria, so this next song is for Maria. I'd also like to dedicate this song to the special someone in my life." Adam grinned. "You know who you are."

Nate caught the surprise on Cade's face and groaned. Damn the man. Everyone else would suspect Adam was talking about a woman. He knew better. He hoped none of the band suspected. Damn, he'd kill Adam when he got his hands on him.

"ARE YOU GONNA SPILL about this special someone in your life?" Morgan demanded once they'd finished the last bracket of songs and completed an encore.

J.T. packed away his guitar and straightened. "Yeah, who is it? I haven't seen you with anyone recently."

Adam regretted saying anything. Nate would be pissed, but hell, he knew what he wanted. He'd thought about it a lot recently. Despite his worries the previous night and this morning, he'd come to a decision. This thing with Nate wasn't a whim on his part. He was a click of fingers away from toppling into love, if he wasn't there already, and he wasn't afraid to admit it. Taking a deep breath, he strove for damage control. "Can't get anything past you guys. I thought if I said there was someone special, the fans might stop throwing themselves at me or trying to sneak into my room like those ones a few months ago. You know what the boss said about staying single. She said it's better for business."

"Who wants to settle down?" Morgan asked. "We have our music and chicks on tap. It's heaven."

Adam shook his head, smirking as Morgan had obviously intended him to. "Don't you get lonely sometimes?"

"How could any of you get lonely?" Nate asked, appearing without warning. "You're the tightest-knit group of guys I've ever worked with. How were the borrowed instruments?"

"Not too bad," Cade said. "At least we have a few days before the next show. I might be able to find a guitar I like."

A knock sounded on the door. Susan, their manager, arrived in a cloud of perfume that reminded Adam of wildflowers.

She shot him a hard look, and he had to stop himself from shifting from foot to foot. He grinned because he knew it would annoy her.

"Who is this special someone?" she demanded.

Adam sauntered across the room, dodging J.T. and Cade to reach her. He slid an arm around Susan's plump shoulders and planted a kiss on her forehead. "It's you, sweetheart. No one else will have me."

"I'm not surprised, if you use that smarmy charm," she countered tartly. "And I notice they didn't let up on the panties. The stage was littered with them when I left."

"You're going to have to arrange for a barricade," Morgan said. "A pair almost got caught in the strings of my guitar tonight."

Susan's eyes glittered with humor. "It might start a

new trend if every second note is muffled by panties. I've arranged a meeting with a couple of guys from the record label tomorrow at the Winston Hotel. Lunch. I want you to turn up bright-eyed and bushy-tailed. No hangovers. Take it easy tonight and make sure you get plenty of sleep." She paused to eye Cade. "Behave tonight," she admonished. "The meeting is important. I want to make a good impression. Understood?"

"Yes, ma'am," Adam said. "We won't let you down." They wouldn't, either, since they all respected Susan and what she'd done for them. While they partied hard, all of them were serious about their music.

"And no more talk of a special someone. Record sales will be better if you're single."

Adam forced himself not to react. He didn't think a female partner would hurt, and there would come a time when one or more of them ignored Susan's stricture. Coming out as a gay, though? Nope, he could see how that might hurt future record sales. People liked to talk about embracing others for who they were, but when it came down to it, they didn't truly believe the words they spouted. He'd learned that the hard way. His parents swore they loved him, yet they'd rejected him quick enough.

"The van's ready and parked out the back," Nate said. "Do you want me and Keith to start loading up now?"

"Please," Cade said.

Adam nodded, grateful for the interruption. When Susan was out of earshot, he said to Cade, "Are you going to stay the night with your girl?"

"Yeah, she's in town again because of her job, so I thought I would. Are you going to be okay on your own?"

"Nate thought it might be better to stay at the new hotel for tonight because the security is better," Adam said.

"Good," Cade said. "Nate won't let anyone get close to you. It was a good day when he signed on with us. I like him."

Adam stared at Nate and watched the play of muscles under his shirt when he lifted an amplifier. "Yeah, he's a good friend. He really saved our butts the other night."

"Did you say something to Susan?"

"Nah, she knows about the thefts. I didn't want to worry her about the other."

Cade nodded. "Yeah, that was my thought. What she doesn't know won't hurt her."

"How about we meet at the hotel tomorrow and go to the lunch meeting together?" Adam asked.

"I'll be there at half past eleven," Cade said. "I'll head off from here tonight."

Adam winked. "Have a good night. I'll let the others know."

121

Cade walked off to help pack up, and Adam did the same. An hour later, Nate and Adam entered their hotel room and shut the door on the rest of the world.

The second the door closed, Adam's heart started to race. His hand trembled when he set his wallet and the van keys on the coffee table.

"You feel like a drink?" Nate asked. "I still have a partial bottle of whiskey."

"Sounds..." Adam paused to clear his throat. "Sounds good." He watched Nate stroll over to his pack and his jeans pull tight across his ass when he bent to retrieve the whiskey. Damn, he was toast. The man pushed every one of his buttons, and the small taste he'd had so far only fueled the simmering lust inside him.

Nate poured whiskey into two glasses and handed one to Adam. He caught Adam's gaze and held it. "Who is the someone special?"

"You have to ask?"

"Yes."

"There's no one in my life apart from you." Adam watched the tide of color crawl across Nate's cheeks, fascinated by the moment of uneasiness and embarrassment. "I'm not interested in anyone else."

"Jesus," Nate muttered. "You had to say something. Why couldn't you keep your mouth shut?"

Adam noticed he didn't deny there was something between them. That was more than he'd hoped for. "I didn't mention names."

"But now everyone is wondering. They'll be watching."

"So we'll save the misbehaving for when we're in private." Adam hoped Nate would feel like misbehaving tonight. He couldn't wait to get his hands on the other man. His gaze swept down Nate's body and slowly returned to his face.

Nate set his glass aside and prowled toward him. Adam felt his eyes widen. He started to set his glass down, but Nate grabbed his shoulders and slammed their mouths together before he could complete the move. The glass toppled to the thick carpet, spilling cold whiskey on his T-shirt on the way to the floor. Adam didn't care because Nate had his arms around him. Their lips moved together. When he groaned, Nate slipped his tongue into his mouth. Damn, that felt good. Adam hadn't thought it would be this easy. He'd been ready to start over, to seduce Nate again, if that was what it took.

This worked much better.

The kiss gentled, sending messages of lust to his groin. He groaned, trembling with his need, wanting Nate's hands and mouth on his skin in the worst way. He craved the physical contact. A demand tickled the tip of his tongue, while a touch of fear tempered impetuous pleas. Vulnerability. Along with loving Nate came susceptibility. He left himself open to a possible world of pain.

Then Nate jerked up his T-shirt, the fumes of the spilled whiskey rising between them. He tossed the garment aside and stared at Adam's chest and shoulder before dipping his head to lick across the spirals of the tattoo on Adam's right biceps. As he worked his way up to Adam's shoulder, Adam swallowed the knot of tension in his throat. It was an innocent touch, but it gave him hope that they could work toward something more advanced.

Adam's stomach muscles tensed at the thought of fucking Nate, the tight heat of his channel clamping down on his cock. "More." The gritty tone hinted at his enjoyment.

Nate stopped and grinned up at him in blatant appraisal. "I've wanted to do that for weeks."

"Oh, yeah? Feel welcome to indulge yourself any time." Hell, didn't Nate realize he had free rein to touch him? "Anything else on your to-do list?"

Nate lifted his head, his eyes bright as he cupped Adam's jaw. "Now that you mention it." He kissed him, this time slow and leisurely, tongues dancing in tormenting strokes until Adam ached with the need to fuck.

Breathing hard, Adam pulled away, desperate to satiate

the agonizing hunger he harbored for this man. Nate watched, his gaze roving over and lingering on his chest, on his shoulder tattoo. It made Adam feel good about his body, glad he kept in shape. He kicked off his boots and rapidly removed the rest of his clothes. Heat licked his skin, each breath labored and fast as if he'd pushed hard during a run.

Adam swallowed before speaking. "Are you going to stand there and stare, or do you want to fool around?"

In seconds flat, Nate stripped. They toppled to the bed, kissing, rubbing their bodies together. It was innocent stuff, but Adam enjoyed every touch, every slide of fingers and silken caress of lips. He let himself go, not bothering to hold back, and when Nate curled his big hand around his cock, pumping firmly, he came, the pleasure a roaring sound in his ears. Even though he craved more from Nate, this was good, and so much better than his imagination.

"Damn, did you have to aim at me?" Nate complained.

Adam laughed, not used to the humor and fun during sex. Usually when he fucked it was furtive and quick. This was much better.

"Your fault." He straddled Nate's legs and grasped the other man's cock. Different than his, longer and not quite as broad. He stroked it, thumbing across the pearl of pre-come that beaded on the tip. He bent his head and licked away the next droplet, letting Nate's taste fill his mouth. Salty and musky. Nate's cock seemed to swell to larger proportions, and when Adam glanced up to study Nate's face, he noticed the shiver that racked his lover's body.

Good. He wasn't alone.

This thing between them, whatever it was, worked both ways.

"Damn, I'm not sure this should feel so good," Nate said, threading his hands through Adam's hair, his hips jerking as Adam swirled his tongue around the swollen head of his dick.

Adam smiled around Nate's cock and continued to suck and tease with his tongue. God, he loved the sounds Nate was making, the rumbles of enjoyment deep in his chest. He gripped Nate's hips, holding him still and working hard to give him every bit of pleasure he was capable of giving. He could almost see the tight coil of desire releasing inside Nate. His large body shuddered, and a strangled moan escaped, louder than before.

"Adam," he gasped, his hips jerking upward, his grip on Adam's head tightening.

Semen blasted into his mouth, not exactly taking him by surprise, but making him work to swallow. Finally, Nate's cock softened and, with a final swipe of his tongue, Adam lifted his head.

"Thank you," Nate said, stroking his hand over Adam's hair.

"I don't expect thanks." He wanted respect and a future with Nate, dammit. He needed to know he was important to Nate. Early days yet. It wouldn't take much to scare off Nate.

Nate stared at him, his sensual mouth pulling to a frown. "I didn't mean to offend you."

"You didn't."

"I want to take things slowly," Nate said.

It was Adam's turn to frown. He moved up the bed, hesitant to crawl into Nate's arms. Before he could decide, Nate stood, pulled back the covers and climbed into the bed, brows rising while he waited for Adam to join him.

Okay, so Nate wasn't calling things off. "What do you mean?"

"It means I *need* to take things slowly. We work together. I like working for you and the rest of the band. I don't want to fuck that up."

"But you want to continue with this? With us?" Adam asked, trying not to panic. He respected Nate for being upfront and actually verbalizing his concerns.

"This being a relationship?"

"Yeah."

"We're friends. I like you, but I still think we should take this slowly. One day at a time. You might change your mind."

Adam thought about that for a moment. "I don't think so."

"Yeah?"

Adam grinned and planted a kiss on Nate's forehead. "Yeah, I know what I want."

Nate turned off the lights, plunging the room into darkness. Adam lay still for a few seconds before edging closer to Nate. When Nate's arms came around him, he smiled. One day at a time. He could deal with the delay for full sexual contact as long as he could fall asleep next to Nate every night.

AT HALF PAST ELEVEN, they met the rest of the band at the hotel.

"Good night?" Cade asked, studying Adam closely.

"Yeah."

"Thought so. You have a hickey on your neck."

"Shit," Adam cursed, pulling his collar up. "That better?"

"Why are you worried?" Cade asked with a lazy grin.

At least he managed to avoid a furtive glance at Nate. "I don't like gossip." And he didn't want to create a situation that might scare Nate into running.

"Then you shouldn't be in the business," J.T. said, clapping him on the back. "You shouldn't be telling the audience about the special someone in your life."

"Who is the lucky lady?" Morgan demanded.

Nate shrugged. "That's what I'd like to know. He won't spill the beans." When the others weren't looking, Nate winked. Warmth spread through Adam, and he had to fight the smile struggling to sneak across his lips. Nate's expression held suitable teasing. No one would suspect them of sharing a bed the previous night and a shower this morning.

"I thought you guys roomed together," Cade said. "Why don't you know?"

One of Nate's brows rose. "You want to play Nancy Drew, you room with him. I was tired and went to sleep."

"We'd better get going," Adam inserted into the conversation before the interrogation grew more heated. "I want to stop at that music shop near the Winston Hotel to check out their guitars. We didn't have a chance to visit there yesterday."

"Do you need us to go with you?" Keith asked.

Adam hesitated, wanting Nate with him, close enough

to touch, wanting Nate to spend the day with the band so they could chat about their time together later on tonight. But he was trapped because he couldn't show the rest of his friends how he felt about Nate. "Nah, you guys can do your own thing until around four this afternoon."

"Let's go," J.T. said. "I'm driving."

Adam hesitated, glanced at Nate and couldn't guess the other man's thoughts. He didn't want to leave, but he didn't have an alternative. Adam allowed the others to hustle him into the van. They drove off, the others excited by the upcoming meeting at the Winston. The excitement and anticipation found an outlet in ribald jokes. They were hooting with laughter by the time they parked and piled out of the van.

"We have an hour before our meeting," Cade said. "Let's hustle."

After a successful shopping trip, they arrived at the hotel in high spirits. Susan met them in the foyer and escorted them into a private dining room, issuing instructions.

"Let me do all the talking," she said. "They want to meet you today. We'll discuss the recording schedule later. Act polite and answer their questions."

J.T. saluted. "Yes, ma'am."

"Don't worry," Adam said. "We want this. We'll be on our best behavior."

God, this was really happening. They were moving up the ladder, and all he could think was that Nate should be here to share the moment.

JUSTIN COVERED LARA'S HAND with his and smiled. He clasped her fingers, savoring her silky skin and basking in her smile. She cocked a brow when he slid from his chair and knelt in front of her.

"Justin?" Her voice held gently inquiry, and she looked like a picture of femininity in a red dress that flowed across her full curves without being tacky. More than ever, Justin knew this was the right decision. He thought she'd say yes, but, as always with Lara, he couldn't predict how she would react. She had a core of steel and didn't approve of some of his lifestyle. In the past, he'd found himself changing his schedule so she'd spend time with him.

She would leave him if she ever found out about the hit on Adam. She'd never find out if he had his way.

He smiled at her, watched her brown eyes widen as if she felt the importance of the moment. "Lara, will you marry me? I love you, and I can't think of anyone I'd rather spend the rest of my life with."

"Marry?" A small pucker marred the smoothness of

her brow. "I didn't realize you were looking for a serious relationship. You never have before."

"I hadn't met you before."

"I noticed that you're not sleeping with as many women." She paused, nibbled her bottom lip. "If we were to marry, I couldn't sanction the idea of other women. I would want you to be faithful to me."

Justin didn't even hesitate. For so long, he'd felt as if he were alone. When he spent time with Lara, the solitary feeling disappeared. "That would be acceptable. I can do my job without bedding other women. Sweetheart, I don't want anyone else except you." He pulled a black velvet ring box from his pocket and opened it to display the ruby and diamond ring. Justin had gone with large and tasteful rather than ostentatious. The sparkle in Lara's brown eyes told him he'd made the right decision. "So you'll marry me?"

"Yes," she whispered. "I can't think of anything better."

Triumphant, Justin extracted the ring from the box and slid it onto Lara's ring finger. "Our marriage will be a time of great celebration." And hopefully it would appease his father and the other elders who held such sway with the rest of the villagers. "I love you, Lara."

He rose to his feet and swept her into his arms to claim a kiss, his hands holding her in a possessive manner that six months ago would have made him laugh. How time changed one's perspective. His mind wandered, a sliver of unease escaping to play havoc with his happiness. Once again his future depended on Adam.

He pulled away from Lara and grinned at her. Turning, he seized a chilled bottle of champagne from an ice bucket. The rush of the sparkling liquid into the glass replaced the tinkle of displaced ice in the bucket. He handed a stemmed glass to Lara with a smile. Picking up his own glass, he lifted it in a toast. "To our love and happiness."

"To our love and happiness." A flush of pleasure colored Lara's cheeks, contrasting with the raven-black hair and the lustrous diamond earrings. *His.* She was beautiful, and he couldn't wait to make love with her. They would make beautiful babies together, and he intended to start on the business of children straightaway. A child would cement his position with both his father and Lara.

They wouldn't want Adam to return then.

CHAPTER SEVEN

THE RUN-THROUGH OF THE song went well, the music pouring from their fingers in a magical wave that seemed to feed on itself. They nailed the song in the Denver studio on the first take. Man, what an adrenaline rush. They started work on the next song, for once everything going just right. The replacement guitars and the saxophone hadn't caused the problems they envisioned. Adam and the others left the studio on a real high.

"Let's celebrate," J.T. said.

"Not too hard," Susan ordered.

"Sure thing, boss," Cade drawled, slinging an arm around her shoulders and giving her a sweaty hug.

"Yuck! Adam, can we have a word before you leave?"

"Adam's in trouble. Whatcha done, Adam?" Morgan

taunted.

Adam shrugged. He had a clear conscience. "Sure thing. I'll meet you guys outside in a few."

"Today went really well," Susan said. "I'm proud of you boys."

"Yes, Mom," Adam said.

Susan made a growling sound deep in her throat.

"Aw, you like us teasing you."

Susan chuckled. "But you're not sure. If you or any of the boys start stepping out of line, you'll hear about it. This is a tough business, and you're only as good as your last recording or concert."

The humor and feel-good mood slipped away from Adam. His mouth firmed to a frown. "Is there a problem?"

"I just wanted to reiterate that you all need to remain single at present. It's important because of the way we intend to market the band. You mentioned someone special in your life."

Fuck. Adam sucked in a quick breath, struggling to hide his panic. The others had warned him, but Nate made him happy. He'd had to say something or risk bursting. But the last thing he wanted to do was shove Nate into the spotlight. "There might be," he admitted cautiously.

"A couple of reporters have contacted me to ask about your girl."

"Can't I have a private life? Why does everyone need to have the details?" Nate would kill him. He was still as jumpy as a man with ants in his pants, and this might send him running. Adam didn't want that. Having Nate around helped to keep him sane.

"Of course you're entitled to a private life." Susan grasped his upper arm and squeezed, a gentle smile on her lips. "But if you want to keep it private, you shouldn't announce teasers during a show."

"Point taken."

"So who is she?"

Adam snorted, trying for the toughest bluff of his life. "Everyone assumed I was talking about a lover, but the fact is the person I had in mind was my grandmother. It was her birthday and she was on my mind."

"You don't talk about your family."

"No." Adam wasn't about to tell Susan of his family history. As far as his family was concerned, he didn't exist, which suited him fine. The last thing he wanted was to land in the middle of Kokopelli business, not when music was his life.

"As I've said, it really is best for the band if you all remain single." Susan paused, waiting for him to say more, but he didn't bite. Silence had never bothered him and, after a while, she continued. "It keeps the girls coming to the concerts."

Adam didn't agree. He'd never agreed, though he didn't want to put Nate in the middle of a media frenzy. "Sure. Whatever."

"Good." Susan scanned his face and what she saw seemed to reassure her. She nodded. "Good. See you tomorrow."

Adam lifted a hand in farewell and strode from the studio building. Nate had parked out front, and the rest of his friends leaned out the window, hollering at him to hurry.

"What did Susan want?" Cade asked when he climbed inside the van.

"Reminding me about our agreement not to have a private life." Adam met Nate's gaze in the rearview mirror and caught the concern, the tightening of his jaw. Damn. He shouldn't have said anything. He should have lied and told them it was a technical issue.

"It was a suggestion," Cade said, his tone defiant, "made at the start of our careers. We have a right to a private life."

"That's what I told her."

The roar of a motorbike and the toot of a vehicle behind filled the bloom of silence in the van. Nate glanced at him again, this time with a faint smile on his full lips. All Adam could think about was getting Nate alone, touching his lips to Nate's until passion replaced his smile and need raced through both of them.

"Cade is serious about his girl," Morgan crowed.

"I'm not."

But Cade was serious. The creep of heat to his cheeks and the need to defend his privacy told Adam the story. "Stop giving him a hard time."

"Yeah," Cade muttered, his gaze switching to shifty. "Besides, we were talking about Adam."

"Where are we celebrating tonight?" Adam asked in a firm voice that had them all hooting with laugher. He caught Nate's smirk, the way he laughed with the others, and immediately decided on sensual payback the next time they were alone.

Keith met them back at the motel, and Adam knew there was something wrong after seeing the taut expression on his face.

"What's up?" Adam asked.

"My father is sick. He's been rushed to hospital in California."

"Man, why didn't you ring us at the studio?" Morgan demanded.

J.T. squeezed his shoulder in sympathy. "Do you have a flight booked?"

"Yeah, I fly out in an hour. I've packed all the gear. It's

138

ready for you to leave for the next gig."

"You should have called," Nate said, his husky voice stirring renewed desire in Adam, despite the circumstances.

"I needed something to do to keep busy," Keith said.

Nate gestured at the van. "Do you want a ride to the airport?"

"That would be great."

"I'll come too," Adam said. "See you guys later."

They dropped Keith at the airport, Adam telling him to take his time coming back, that they'd manage without him.

A camera flashed in their faces as they walked out of the airport to the car park, the photographer hurrying after them to ask questions about their recent signing. Adam paused to answer the man's questions, hiding his impatience when all he wanted was to spend time with Nate.

"Last question," Adam stated finally, grinning to take any sting from his words. "We have a gig to rehearse for."

"I know. I have a ticket for your next concert. Last question—who is the special someone in your life?"

Adam forced a smile, wishing again that he hadn't opened his big mouth. "People keep asking me that. It's my grandmother."

139

"Your grandmother?" The photographer looked disappointed as he glanced at Nate for confirmation.

"It's true," Nate said. "Everyone thinks it's Adam's girl."

"Gran is my girl," Adam said firmly. Hopefully, they wouldn't delve into his past too hard. Most of his official past bore little resemblance to the truth. "Thanks for the chat." Adam lifted his hand in a farewell wave and headed toward the van. Nate fell into step.

"Did you really tell Susan it was your grandmother?"

"I did. Should I have told her the truth?"

"Susan is your manager. You trust her."

"With business stuff. Yeah. She's not our keeper and she has no power to control our personal lives, despite what we agreed to at the start when she took us on or what she's telling us now." Adam heard the sharp note in his voice and grinned, trying to take some of the acid away. He didn't want to discuss this. All he wanted was to go back to their room and get naked with Nate. He hoped like hell that was what Nate wanted too.

"Whatever. Do you feel as if someone is watching us?"

Adam glanced over his shoulder. "The reporter is staring at us still."

"No, it's not the reporter. The back of my neck is itching." Nate unlocked the van and climbed behind the wheel. "Never mind. Chalk it down to a good imagination."

"Does that imagination extend to the bedroom?"

Nate's lips twisted as he backed out of the parking space and drove toward the exit. "That's for me to know and you to find out."

"Fighting words."

"Don't forget it," Nate said lightly.

It made Adam conjure all sorts of scenarios. His lips curled, while other parts of his body tightened with anticipation. "You know I'm gonna call you on it later."

Nate shot him a look and winked. "I'm countin' on it."

"If we can find some private time," Adam added.

"With Keith gone, we probably need one less hotel room. Cade spends most of his time with his lady since she's based in Denver, which leaves us in a room together without sneaking around."

"You've given this some thought."

"You've unleashed a monster."

Adam smirked and blew him a kiss. For the rest of the drive, they talked about their move to another town for a new gig and the songs Adam was working on to add to their repertoire.

"You inspire me."

"Me?" Nate said.

"Yeah, I haven't written so many songs for ages. Cade

and Morgan asked me what was wrong with me this morning. Why do you keep looking in the mirror?"

"There's a car behind us. If I didn't know better, I'd swear they're following. The driver has taken every turn I've made."

Adam twisted to study the vehicles behind them. "Are you sure? It's probably a coincidence."

"Maybe. You have to admit, some weird things have happened in the last two months. The attack and the break-in at the hotel." Nate pulled up outside the hotel and parked the van in their usual spot. "You're probably right and it's nothing."

"We'll mention it to the others. If we all keep an eye on our surroundings, we'll soon notice if there's something weird. Maybe it's an overzealous fan."

Nate shook his head as he brushed past a leafy shrub that seemed to have gone mad in the last week with a frantic growth spurt. "Nah, if it was a fan, they'd make a point of saying hello. Don't worry. It's probably my imagination."

※※※※※ ※※※※※

ANOTHER TOWN, ANOTHER PUB. Another cheap Colorado hotel. After helping the band set up for the coming evening, Nate took a seat and watched them do a sound check and run through a couple of the new numbers. Unbidden, his gaze went to Adam. Since Keith had left, they'd barely managed more than a quick kiss. He hadn't realized he'd miss the closer contact with Adam, actively crave it the way he had. Not being able to touch Adam was slowly driving him crazy.

The notes of the song drifted to a close, the smoky tones of Adam's voice curling through him in a manner that made his jeans feel tight and uncomfortable. Nate stood and moved so a strategic chair hid his groin from the band members. Then he caught Adam's smirk. His mouth tightened, opened to say something before snapping shut again. The words on the tip of his tongue weren't for public consumption.

"I'll meet you back here for the gig," Cade said. "I'm meeting Maggie's parents tonight since they've come from Montana to visit her. I won't be back at the hotel later, either," he added to Nate. "Don't wait up."

"You're like a clumsy ox stumbling around in the dark. You wake us up every time," Adam said.

"Hey, I can be quiet," Cade protested.

"Nope." Nate shook his head. "I've yet to see it."

"Don't you mean hear it?" J.T. asked, grinning. "Why do you think I chose to room with Morgan?"

"Well, you could have mentioned it to us," Adam said.

"I'm not listening to this denigration of my good character," Cade said. "Catch you later tonight."

Nate and the others walked outside to the van. As soon as they exited the pub, the hair on the back of his neck prickled. It wasn't his imagination. He'd thought someone had followed them from the hotel, yet he hadn't glimpsed anything or anyone out of the ordinary. An overactive imagination, he'd decided. Now he wasn't so sure. Eyes watched them. He'd stake his life on it.

"Hurry," he barked at J.T. and Morgan.

J.T. shot him a look of surprise. "Who lit the fire in your britches?"

"I'm starving," Nate said.

"Me too," Adam agreed, and Nate let a breath ease out when his lover climbed inside the van. This preternatural awareness had something to do with Adam. He didn't like the weird things that had happened and wasn't about to ignore his instincts this time.

Back at the hotel, Nate ordered chili con carne and cornbread and added salads in the interest of a balanced menu. They met up in Nate and Adam's room and, to Nate's intense frustration, seemed inclined to linger. No way did he intend to invite them for drinks later tonight.

"Hell, look at the time," he said suddenly. An hour for them to shower, change and get back to the pub. Their room cleared magically. Nate closed the door and locked it before turning slowly to face Adam. "We haven't had much time alone recently."

"Is that a complaint?" Adam tugged off his boots and socks so he was barefoot like Nate.

"A statement."

"What did you have in mind?"

Nate's heart lurched, fear taking a grip before he could shake it off. "A kiss?" The words came out as a distinct question. Damn, he didn't know what he was doing when it came to Adam. Oh, he knew what he wanted, but the directions to get to his destination were murky. He felt as if he wandered, lost in the badlands.

"A kiss I can do," Adam said, his agreeable tone helping Nate relax and stretch his imagination to more than a kiss.

"Maybe a quick shower together and a bit of a grope before we leave? That's all we'll have time for."

Adam's nimble fingers started to unbutton his shirt. "I like the way you think."

Nate stared, eyeing the golden skin Adam revealed with each release of a button. He shrugged it off his shoulders and let the shirt drop to the floor. The rest of his clothes followed. Nate was lost, his emotions more entangled with Adam than he cared to admit. He was falling for the other man and knew it, despite his continuing reservations.

"Are you gonna shower in your clothes?"

"What? No!" Nate dragged his T-shirt over his head and followed Adam to the shower. Mesmerized, he watched the flex of Adam's buttocks as he leaned into the shower to turn on the water. With trembling fingers, Nate unfastened his jeans and pushed them down, maneuvering carefully past his erection. By the time he'd undressed, Adam was already inside the cubicle, ducking his head under the water momentarily before staring at him through spiky dark lashes. Nate stepped inside, walking into his arms and breathing in Adam's scent with a sense of rightness.

"Tonight," Adam breathed before he took possession of his mouth. Firm lips caressed his, the touch seeming to zip straight to his groin.

God, he loved kissing Adam. Those lips that sang so sweetly kissed with real passion, teasing a groan from him. Hands wandered, stroked and squeezed. Wrapped around his dick. The air hissed out of Nate in a laugh while his pulse rate spiked in anticipation.

"We don't have time to do this."

Adam laughed. "Yeah, we do. You're the driver and I'm the lead singer. They can't go without us."

"But—"

Adam sank to his knees in front of Nate and grinned up

at him. "However, I'm gonna move this along because it's unprofessional for me to be late."

And when it came to music, Adam took things seriously. Nate moved a fraction so the water didn't hit Adam in the face.

"You know, I don't want to be furtive and quick about his." Adam changed his mind, stood to grab the soap. "After the concert, okay? You and me. A room without Cade. Privacy."

"Sounds great." And it did. Nate clasped the back of Adam's head. Their bodies rubbed together, wet skin gliding seductively. Nate liked the way Adam's dark lashes fluttered closed when he directed Adam's mouth to his. Their breath mingled, and a hushed moan emerged from Adam seconds before their lips met. Adam's taste was addictive, filling Nate with a yearning for even closer physical contact. When he lifted his head, they were both breathing hard, their erections brushing.

Temptation. It rippled through Nate, making him long to pounce, to force Adam against the wall of the shower cubicle and take his pleasure.

"Later," Adam whispered. "Know that every song I sing tonight is for you."

A chill worked through Nate, despite the spray of warm water pouring down over their bodies. "Later," he confirmed, wondering when Adam had managed to supplant Rosa in his memories.

CHAPTER EIGHT

THE HANDS OF THE clock showed it was well after midnight by the time they arrived back at the hotel. Adam climbed from the van and stretched, holding his hands at the small of his back, his mouth cracked open in a wide yawn.

"No wonder you don't have a date," Morgan said. "That's as attractive as hell."

"Huh! How many pairs of lacy panties did you have chucked at you tonight?" Adam chuckled, knowing he'd have Morgan beat hands down.

"I have a date," Morgan countered, his grin telling Adam to beat that.

"I'm so tired, I doubt I could get it up," Nate said. "Adam snores. Any woman who dates him should get a warning."

J.T. and Morgan hooted at that.

"I've heard Viagra cures a limp dick," Adam said.

"I'm too tired to even argue about it," Nate said, taking off his hat and lifting it in a gesture of farewell. "I'll see you guys tomorrow."

"What are you gonna do?" Adam asked J.T. He had to force himself not to stare at Nate's butt as the man walked away.

"I'm gonna grab a beer and veg in front of the tube."

Adam nodded. "Sounds like a plan. Maybe I'll do the same thing."

"Come to our room," J.T. said.

"Nah, I'm pretty tired too. I'll watch the TV in my room. That way, if I fall asleep, I can do it in comfort. See you tomorrow." Adam trailed after Nate, having a hard time keeping to a walk instead of breaking into a jog. Anticipation thrummed inside him, and outside their room, he fumbled for his key, dropping it on the ground in his haste. The outside light had blown and it didn't make finding his key easy. He cursed softly, retrieving the key and shoving it in the keyhole. The door jerked open before he could turn the key, spilling light over the flourishing green shrub right beside their room.

He sent Nate a sheepish smile. "I dropped my key and

couldn't find it in the dark."

Nate waited until he stepped inside and turned the lock. He'd stripped off his shirt, and Adam's eyes followed the tanned skin, the bulging muscles and the lightly furred chest. His finger itched to touch, and he wanted to taste and lick Nate's flat nipples to hard peaks.

Nate's chuckle jerked Adam back to the present. Color instantly invaded his face, and he thanked his parents for his golden-toned skin that didn't give away his embarrassment easily. "What?" he asked, pretending innocence.

"You're looking at me as if you want to eat me for supper."

"And what if I said that's exactly what I would like?"

"You're not worried that getting closer to me is a bad thing? I don't want you to get hurt."

Adam stared at Nate in surprise. "Don't you mean you're worried about you getting hurt?"

"That too," Nate agreed. "Everything is happening so fast. If people learn that you...that we..." He trailed off in obvious discomfort.

"If they find out I'm queer or that we have a relationship, then they'll have to deal with it. I'm not going to apologize for being with you, for preferring men to women. I'm not going to give you up because some people think an intimate relationship between two men is not God's will."

"What about J.T., Morgan and Cade? What will they think?"

Adam frowned, not liking the direction of this conversation. "I don't know what they'll think. We could tell them and find out." Why the hell was Nate trying to put distance between them? "Nate, if you have a problem, tell me. If something is worrying you, spit it out. We can't fix a problem if I don't know about it."

"I..." Nate's shoulders slumped momentarily before lifting again. "No problem. Just tired, I guess."

Adam sensed he was lying, but he couldn't push too hard. No matter what he said or how hard he pretended to himself, he knew the truth. Nate was the one for him. He didn't want another man. He definitely did not want a woman. "Why don't you go to sleep? I'm gonna grab a beer and watch TV for a while. I'm still high from the show."

"It was a great show," Nate said. "'Alone' will be a huge hit."

"I don't have a grandmother. You know that, right? Every time I sing 'Alone', it's for you." His voice broke in an unmanly croak toward the end of his sentence, emotion getting the better of him. Nothing less than the truth, though. He didn't intend to lie to Nate.

A strange expression flashed across Nate's face. Adam

didn't know whether it was pleasure or shock or something in between. It made him hesitate, suddenly unsure. Had he read more into this relationship than he should have? He knew Nate still thought about his wife a lot. It was only natural. Nate didn't screw around. He'd known that, admired it, but he had to admit it was difficult to fight a dead woman. And kinda sad on his part that he thought of Rosa as a competitor.

"That's dangerous. What if an enterprising reporter or fan decides to dig into your family tree?"

Adam shrugged and hoped he managed to hide the sliver of fear that snaked down his spine. Nate was right. He didn't want anyone knowing about his past, and since he hadn't hidden his real name and still used it, an enterprising snoop might strike gold and hit on information about his background or the hundred-pound gorilla that lurked in his closet along with his sexuality. Most people were uneasy in the presence of the supernatural. Kokopelli definitely resided in the supernatural section. And if he continued his relationship with Nate, he probably should tell him. Maybe.

"What? What's wrong?" Nate frowned, tension rippling through his upper body.

"Nothing. You're right."

Nate's brows rose. "I am?"

"Yeah."

"That would be a first." Nate unfastened his trousers and slid them down his long legs, then pulled back the covers of the bed he'd been sleeping in for the last couple of days.

Damn, Nate really did intend to go to sleep. Adam shoved aside the physical desire crawling through his gut. The last thing he wanted was for Nate to think he was sex-mad, no matter how close that was to the truth. A grimace distorted his face as he sauntered over to the fridge and snagged a bottle of beer. "Will the television keep you awake?"

"Nah, I'm so tired I could sleep through anything." To illustrate his point, his mouth opened in a wide yawn as he crawled between the sheets.

Yup, no sex tonight, Adam thought glumly.

Ten minutes later, Nate's deep breaths told Adam he was asleep. Adam finished his beer and decided he'd crawl into bed with Nate. If they couldn't have sex, at least they could sleep close, hold each other.

Without giving it another thought, Adam switched off the light, stripped and slipped under the covers. The heat emanating from Nate drew him in, and Adam settled his body against Nate's, sighing in contentment. There was no other place he'd rather be.

Someone woke him, hours later or it could have been minutes.

"I don't remember inviting you into my bed," a familiar husky voice said.

Adam cuddled closer without opening his eyes, savoring the soft texture of Nate's chest hair, his muscled thigh sliding between his legs. "I wanted to be near you."

"Yeah?"

"That's right. Do you have a problem with that?" Adam wriggled closer, unabashedly rubbing his cock against Nate's leg.

"What am I going to do with you?"

"Fuck me?" Adam said, hearing the hopeful note in his voice and not caring if it gave away his vulnerability and need.

"That could be arranged."

"Good, but you're wearing too many clothes."

Nate laughed and wriggled out of his boxer-briefs. "That better?"

The feel of skin on skin made Adam groan out loud. "Hell, yeah." Blindly he reached for Nate, searching for his mouth and finding it in a fierce clashing of lips. Rough stubble and softer beard hair abraded his cheek, his mouth. Nate's taste filled him, and with it came the joy of feeling wanted. It hit him in that instant how right this felt, loving Nate. He wrapped his arms around the other man, thrusting his hips and shuddering because it felt so good. Before he knew it, they were rocking against each other, gasps and moans filling the air. Hands stroked, teeth nipped and the pleasure grew as they moved together. Adam reached between them, grasping both cocks in his hand, firmly pumping until his balls were so hard he thought they might burst. A final hard stroke and he exploded, his belly muscles tensing as his dick jerked with the force of his release.

"Damn," Nate muttered, his breathing loud in Adam's ear.

The splash of semen against his chest made him ease back on the hand action. Nate shuddered against him. Adam kissed Nate again, this time slowly, putting everything he felt and couldn't say into the kiss. When he finally pulled away, they were both breathing hard.

Adam forced himself to move. "I'll get a cloth." It was best he left before he said something he shouldn't, admitted his love and put real pressure on their fragile relationship.

In the bathroom, he gave himself a swift lecture, his eyes bleary in the bright light. Grabbing a cloth, he turned on the tap and waited for it to run hot. Then his eyes widened and a gasp escaped. The Kokopelli mark on his chest. After he'd left the village, cast out by his father and the other villagers, the tattoo, for want of a better word, had faded until only he knew where it had once been. But now it was returning. It was much darker, dark enough that Nate would see it and ask questions. The rest of the band would notice if he removed his shirt.

Frowning, he swiped the stickiness from his chest and refreshed the cloth for Nate. What did this mean? Had something happened to his brother? Hell! No way did he want to return to the village to carry out the Kokopelli duties. He couldn't give up his music. Damn, he refused. Music had saved him once, and these days he lived to play with the band, to sing and write his songs. He'd never return to the village to face the narrow-minded people from his childhood because that would mean giving up Nate.

Deep in troubled thought, he switched off the light, paused to let his eyes adjust and returned to Nate. When Nate reached for the cloth, he slapped his hand away. "No, let me. I like touching you."

Nate didn't argue, but merely relaxed back onto the mattress and waited for Adam to cleanse his chest. "Are you going to let me back into your bed?"

"Now?"

"Yeah, I want to sleep with you."

157

Nate snorted and shifted over a fraction. "Somehow, I don't think I have an option. You'll just creep back once I go to sleep."

"Probably. Besides, Cade isn't here. When he's here, we don't have the opportunity to sleep together. I miss it." He smirked suddenly. "I sure as hell won't grieve over skipping my turn to sleep on the rollaway bed."

"There's always the next stop. Okay, but the minute you start snoring or try to push me out of bed, you're outta here," Nate warned.

Adam grinned. Somehow he didn't think Nate meant that. He tossed the cloth aside, dragged the covers over them and snuggled against Nate's slightly larger frame. He could have easily gone another round, but Nate was already close to sleep, each of his breaths coming slow and steady. Adam grinned and closed his eyes, soaking in the other man's closeness and his scent. Plenty of time for sex. Relaxed and warm, he started to think about music, lyrics for a new song drifting through his mind. He fell asleep halfway through the second verse.

The slide of a key in the lock and a soft curse woke him. Half-awake, Adam took longer than usual to process the sounds.

"Fuck," Cade muttered.

The distinct thunk told Adam that Cade had walked

into the table. He threw back the covers, ready to scramble into his bed, but the sudden flare of the light stole the stealthy option from him.

"Fuck," Cade said again, this time in shock.

Adam shot a guilty glance at Nate and saw he was awake and fully alert, his inscrutable expression doing little to indicate how Adam should react.

"You're in bed together," Cade said. "Naked."

Give the man a prize. Adam wanted to curse a blue streak and then do it again. Too late. "What are you doing here? I thought you were meeting us at the studio." A flick of his wrist yanked the covers over to screen his nakedness.

"Don't try to change the subject. How long has this been going on?"

"It's private," Adam said, instinctively knowing if he didn't handle this situation carefully, Nate would leave. That was the last thing he wanted.

Cade plonked onto a chair, making himself comfortable. It didn't look as if he was leaving anytime soon, not without answers.

"Can you at least make some coffee and give us a chance to get dressed?" Adam snapped, not holding back on his temper. Nate leaving would really piss him off.

With a nod, Cade stood. "Sure. I'll go and get some breakfast from the diner."

"Put the coffee on first," Nate said, his first words giving Adam hope. They didn't sound like the words of a man who intended to run.

They waited in taut silence while Cade filled the coffeemaker with water and ripped open the packet of coffee grinds, cursing under his breath when he spilled some. Adam swallowed and closed his eyes. He could feel the heat coming off Nate's body, the other man so close they were almost touching. Almost. In this case, almost seemed like a hundred miles, with uncertainty filling the distance between.

Cade's boots thudded on the tile floor before the cheap carpet muffled the sound. At the door, he paused. "See you in a few. We'll talk," he added before closing the door behind him.

In the silence that Cade left behind, Adam waited for the axe to fall, to hack away the happiness he'd found with Nate.

"Do you think he'll tell the others?" Nate asked, still not moving.

"I don't know." Fear kept Adam from looking at Nate again. "At least he didn't throw a spastic fit and tell us we're sick."

"Adam."

When fear kept Adam from turning to look at him, Nate

took the lead and slid close, pushing him flat on his back. Nate leaned over, staring down with a serious mien. "This is the last thing I wanted to happen, but I'm not ashamed of being with you. Finding a connection with another person is difficult. Friendship should always be treasured."

"Is that all this is to you? Friendship?" Hurt and a hint of anger layered each word of his abrupt retort. Adam knew if he could hear the underlying fear, Nate would have no difficulty in discerning the emotion. That irritated him. He didn't want to come across as needy. He'd done fine on his own so far.

"It's more than friendship, and you know it. Don't act like a baby." The flash of Nate's impatience turned Adam on even as he winced inwardly at the inherent sting. Nobody liked the label of childish.

"What do you want to tell Cade? The rest of the band? You know them better than me. How will they react to us being together?"

Nate's questions relaxed the ball of tension in his gut, and Adam melted into the mattress in a play at calm. "I'm not ashamed of who I am. I'm more worried about you. Will you leave?" *More important, will you leave me?*

"You're not answering my questions. How will the band react?"

"I'm not sure. We've never discussed the gay issue,

mainly because I didn't want to know what they thought."
He forced a confident smile, not wanting to alarm Nate.
"It'll be all right. They're my friends. We've been together
for years."

"But you're not sure."

"How can I really be sure until I tell them?" A tremor
slipped through his body at the thought. Fear. Damn, he
was worried about their reaction. And Cade would tell
them. He knew that without a shred of doubt.

"Did you know Cade was coming back this morning?
Did you orchestrate this?"

"Fuck, no!" Adam snapped, incensed at the accusation.
"I would never do something so underhanded. There's no
need to insult me."

Nate blinked, the only reaction Adam noticed. He
wasn't sure if Nate believed him or not. "We'd better move
before Cade gets back."

Nate pushed away, lifting the covers in the process. He
paused, a frown on his face as he stared at Adam's chest.
"When did you get the Kokopelli tattoo? It wasn't there
yesterday." He traced it with a forefinger, the sensual drag
of a callused finger against his flesh making Adam's body
react. A groan emerged, low and throaty. A distinctly
sexual jolt pulsed through him.

"I..." Adam swallowed. "Do that again. Touch it again."

Nate traced the outline of the Kokopelli with his finger, finally raising his gaze in a question. "It's not a new tattoo, because there's no inflammation of your skin. It's not a temporary tat, either."

"I...no, it's not. Can we talk about it later? Please?"

Nate's eyes narrowed. "Tonight after the show. We'll get a hotel room where we can talk without any interruptions."

"That sounds good." Adam crawled from the bed and grabbed a pair of jeans. The sound of the key in the door made him decide not to look for underwear. Instead, he scrambled into the jeans and zipped them up, leaving the button at the top unfastened. Recalling the emerging Kokopelli on his chest, he donned a T-shirt as well.

"I met the others in the diner," Cade said from the doorway. J.T. grabbed the door so Cade could enter without fumbling and dropping their breakfast. Morgan followed behind, bringing a whiff of fresh air and flowers from the outdoors. Adam frowned at the flowering shrub outside the door before Morgan shut it, blocking his view. With a sense of foreboding, he watched his friends as they settled around the small table, each claiming a chair.

Shit, the entire band intended to interrogate him and Nate. Nothing like a lynching party to start the day. Adam glanced at Nate, noticed the faint tightening of his mouth, the tense shoulders as he pulled a wrinkled black T-shirt over his head.

Still scowling, Nate strode to the coffeemaker and grabbed cups from the cupboard. He poured coffee for all of them and set the coffeemaker going again without uttering a word.

Adam sighed at the uncomfortable silence, anger starting to build inside him. He was still the same person as he was the day before. So he and Nate slept together. They were discreet and didn't force their relationship down anyone's throat. The guys had no right to judge them.

"What's for breakfast?" he growled.

"Hotcakes," Cade said.

"Thanks." Adam grabbed one of the boxes and syrup, before heading over to a blue couch, since the others occupied all the chairs around the table. He shoved Nate's Stetson aside to make room for someone else to join him if they wanted.

After a swift glance at him, Nate topped up his coffee and strode over to sit next to him. Nate's solid presence helped calm his nerves, but he still felt like a teenager again, facing his father's disapproval. Yeah, and he'd thought he'd left condemnation behind at his family home. His stomach churned afresh. Obviously not. Maybe that's where he'd made his mistake. Lack of openness. Although he'd left home, he hadn't left the closet at the same time, meaning he still walked in murky darkness filled with secrets.

Pissed at the silence, he delivered the opening salvo. "Anyone gonna comment?"

Like a pack of wolves, they attacked, all talking at once.

"Did Cade really catch you in bed together?" J.T. demanded.

"Are you gay?" Morgan's contribution.

"Are the two of you serious about each other, or were you drunk?" Cade's question.

Adam sucked in a deep breath and didn't check Nate's reaction this time. Time for him to man up. Although he didn't intend to shout his sexual orientation to the rooftops—Susan wouldn't like it, for a start—there was no reason why he couldn't discuss the matter with his friends. But if they behaved badly, then all bets were off. There was no way he intended to take crap or let Nate take the brunt of something that was essentially his problem. He'd started this by making a move on Nate.

"I'm gay. It's the reason I left home. My father kicked me out when he discovered I preferred men to women." He spun a censored version of the truth, pinning each of his friends with a stony stare, silently daring them to take potshots.

"Why didn't you say something?" Morgan asked. "I don't care what you do with your sex life, as long as it's legal and you don't bring Stampede bad publicity because of it."

"It's not something I'm comfortable talking about," Adam admitted. "Most people aren't very understanding when it comes to being different. They say they understand, but deep down they're panicking in case the bad gene rubs off on them or their families. Why do you think I was asked to leave home?" Adam swallowed, thinking the past shouldn't still have the power to hurt him this way.

But it was easy to recall the appalled expressions on the villagers' faces when they realized he was gay. They'd worried their unborn children would have the same tendencies because he was Kokopelli, the one who guaranteed fruitful crops, the one who had the power to ensure women conceived to carry on the line.

As if to remind him of the past pain, the Kokopelli tattoo that had reappeared on his chest started to itch and burn. With trembling hands, Adam set his coffee mug on the glass-topped table in front of him and rubbed the tattoo, hoping to alleviate the pain.

"You okay?" Nate murmured.

"Yeah."

A frown puckered Nate's brow, his gaze dropping to Adam's chest. Adam let his hand fall away, not wanting to answer questions now. When Nate opened his mouth, Adam sent him a pleading look. His mouth firmed, his eyes narrowing a fraction, but he dipped his head in a curt nod, silently promising to hold his questions.

"We're not most people," Cade said. "We're friends. Hell, we might as well be family, given the amount of time we spend together."

"So finding me in bed with Nate doesn't bother you?" Adam felt Nate's slight flinch and reached for his hand without even considering their audience.

Nate cursed and stood, ignoring his gesture. "I'm going for a run." He grabbed some gear from his bag and stalked to the bathroom, leaving Adam at the mercy of his friends. Perhaps this was better. He could talk to them without censoring. He and Nate would talk later tonight in private. Hopefully Nate didn't intend to bail on him, because that would break his heart. With the appearance of the Kokopelli tattoo, he needed someone in his corner.

Adam applied himself to breakfast, and the others took the hint, with Cade rising to top up their coffee cups.

"I'll be about an hour," Nate said. "I'll be back in time to drive you to the studio." The door closed behind him and, taking that for a signal, his friends started to talk all at once again.

Adam held up his right hand. "Stop. Let me talk. I like Nate. I really like him, and have for a long time. If you guys scare him off, I'm never gonna forgive you. Give me a hard time if you have a problem, but don't take it out on Nate."

"Adam," J.T. said. "You've been happy lately. We've all noticed it in your performances. You're churning out some great new songs. If you weren't pulling your weight, we'd have grounds to complain."

"Yeah, we're not saying we want to watch you and Nate do it, but you don't have to hide from us," Morgan said, glancing at the others as he spoke.

"You didn't walk in on them," Cade said. "I had to scrub my eyeballs."

"We weren't doing anything." Adam glared at Cade until he noticed the humor lurking in the other man's eyes. "Aw, hell. I walked into that one. It's true, though. We were asleep."

"That's what he says," Cade teased, and Adam knew then that everything would be all right with the band. Business as usual, as long as Nate didn't have an issue with the other guys knowing about their relationship.

THE SLAP OF NATE'S sneakers on the pavement kept company with his whirring thoughts. The band knew. It was the start of an avalanche, and he wasn't even sure what *this* was between him and Adam. He knew he liked the man, admired his talent and drive. He liked the sex and the fact that Adam was letting him set the pace. Not once had Adam complained because they hadn't gone all the way yet. Hell, he'd liked waking up in Adam's arms this morning, which was why he hadn't moved as soon as he'd woken and Cade had discovered them. Adam made him forget Rosa, and that was the part he hated. The way he had to search his mind to produce a mental picture and strain to hear the echoes of her laughter. Rosa... Damn, he'd loved her so much, and now the first person he turned to when he had a thought to share was Adam.

A fool couldn't miss the signs. He'd started to care for Adam.

Nate increased his speed, trying to outrun his thoughts. Didn't work. They followed right along with him, back to the hotel. Sweat dripped down his forehead and shone on his torso by the time he ran through the parking lot, heading to his room. Instead of the trepidation he should feel, anticipation filled him, and that's when he knew it was too late to run.

Adam had already tagged his heart, and he was it.

When he reached the entrance to the hotel, he slowed to a brisk walk. The flowers growing in the terracotta tubs bordering the path were ablaze with varying shades of red. Pausing by one of the tubs, Nate ran through a quick series of stretches before he knocked on their door. "It's me," he called when he heard footsteps.

The door cracked open a fraction. The sense of being watched hit him, bringing a frown. A fan? A reporter? Or someone else?

When the back of his neck prickled again, he turned casually, rolling his shoulders in another stretch. The sense of scrutiny persisted, and when Adam opened the door to let him inside, he entered quickly, relaxing only when the solid wood of the door closed out the rest of the world.

"I keep getting the sense that someone is watching us. Have you felt anything? Seen anyone hanging around?"

Adam wrinkled his nose, and Nate wasn't sure if it was the question or the way he smelled after the run.

"Now that you mention it, I have felt as if we're being watched. I figured it was a fan. Are you okay?" His hand hovered over Nate's arm before falling to his side. Adam's uncertainty pulled at him. Nate knew exactly how he felt, exactly what he was asking.

He opened his mouth to tell Adam it was gonna be all right, but he couldn't. Not when he wasn't sure. "I'm gonna take a shower."

"Okay."

They exchanged a look, holding gazes for a long moment. Each wanted to say something—that was obvious. Nate couldn't find the words, didn't want to confront what he felt for Adam. He walked away, paused. "Have you showered yet?"

"No."

"We could share."

"We could do that," Adam said, his tone instantly lighter. Happier.

Nate nodded and kept walking, his lips quirking in the beginnings of a grin. He'd scarcely flipped on the shower and stripped off his sweaty T-shirt when Adam walked in wearing not a stitch of clothing. His cock drew Nate's attention straightaway, the air hissing from him as a frisson of anticipation hit.

"I want you." The words fell from his mouth unbidden, and embarrassment heated his cheeks.

"Good, I thought Cade and the others might scare you away."

"I...no." But he wasn't sure what he was doing. With Rosa, he'd known exactly what to do, what he'd wanted. He'd found himself thinking about her all the time, wanting to spend every minute of his day with her so he'd asked her to marry him. After they'd married, the feeling between them had deepened. Nate felt the same about Adam, and the intimacy scared him.

"You know we don't have time to do anything except shower?" The amusement in Adam's voice finally forced Nate to look directly at his lover. "But maybe we'll get to the good stuff tonight after we talk." He stepped into the shower, standing to one side to give Nate room. "Turn around. I'll do your back."

The tattoo on Adam's chest caught his attention again, the lines crisp and defined as the water poured down over his head. Questions formed on his lips, but they died when he caught Adam's evasive expression. Nate opened his mouth and closed it again. It was just a tattoo. Nothing sinister in the scheme of things, not compared to people firing guns at them.

"Hurry, Nate. Do you want the others to find us in the shower?"

"Hell, no." The questions would have to come later. Nate turned and presented his back, groaning under his breath as Adam started washing him. Broad hands and callused fingers stroked down his spine, shooting pleasure through him. Blood sank into his groin, his cock rising to the occasion. His next groan was even louder.

"Turn around," Adam whispered into his ear. "I'll do

your front."

Nate obeyed, the air hissing past his lips when Adam's fingers skimmed his cock. "I thought we didn't have time for sex."

Adam slipped to his knees in front of Nate and grinned up at him. "I lied. We have time for a quickie." Before Nate could protest, Adam's lips tightened around him and sucked hard. Primed as he was already by Adam's touch, the mouth action was like a bolt of lightning streaking through him. On unsteady legs, he braced his hands on the side of the shower stall, head bowed to watch the way his cock slid in and out of Adam's mouth. It was the sexiest thing he'd ever experienced, the raw pleasure scraping his nerve endings while water rained down and Adam's appreciative grunts vibrated around his shaft.

"Damn, Adam. You make me crazy."

Adam pulled back and sent him a teasing glance. "In a good way, I hope?"

"Too good." And that was the truth. It was part of the problem—the way Adam replaced memories of Rosa. What kind of a man did that make him? Was he shallow?

"Hey. I'm not trying to replace Rosa. I can't, but I can spend time with you. Be a friend."

"Is that what we are? Friends?" And was he that transparent when he thought about Rosa?

"I hope so. Now be quiet while I get busy. We don't have much time."

Guilt pushed at Nate, but the strong suction of Adam's mouth drove it to the shadows. He held still for as long as he could, letting the pressure build until his entire body shuddered. Then his hips jerked, driving his shaft deep. The heaviness in his balls grew, and he couldn't hold back any longer. With a rough cry, he released, hard spasms rippling the length of his cock as Adam's mouth and tongue worked around him.

Gradually, his cock softened, and Adam rose. Nate wrapped his arms around him and held tight, knowing everything was changing, his world shifting, and all he could do was hang on for the ride.

CHAPTER NINE

GUILT GNAWED AT JUSTIN. He had everything he wanted now. He'd married a wonderful woman who made him forget every other. His father and the other elders had stopped talking about replacing him. They no longer met in secretive huddles or glanced at him with disapproval. An air of confidence filled the villagers, and no one had noticed his tattoo, or, rather, the lack of one. Certainly, Lara hadn't mentioned anything, and he took care not to take off his shirt when anyone else could see him and start speculating.

Now that he no longer felt like a cornered rat, he regretted putting the contract out on Adam.

"What's wrong, Justin?" Lara whispered.

He started, covering it with a rich chuckle. "I didn't hear

you enter the room."

Her hands, tiny yet surprisingly strong, started to knead his shoulder and neck muscles. The tension leached out of him, a groan of pleasure escaping as Lara worked on a knotted muscle.

"That feels good." Too good. Already a hard ridge of flesh pressed against his linen trousers. "The rest of my afternoon is free. We could have a siesta."

"We could, my husband." Her strong fingers dug into a muscle near the base of his neck. "As soon as you tell me what troubles you."

Justin sighed, fear that he might lose her filling him, replacing the ease her touch brought. Yet the knowledge of what he'd done ate at him like a destructive caterpillar destroying a crop. Slowly, he turned to face her. His head bowed in shame, and the emotions weren't a pretense. His behavior truly appalled him. A pity his conscience hadn't come knocking a fraction earlier.

"I've done something." The words rolled from him, becoming easier once he'd started. "I paid an assassin to kill my brother."

The fingers at his neck clenched, nails gouging before they jerked from his back. "You did what?"

Slowly, he turned to face Lara. The condemnation on her face almost destroyed him, and he realized he'd risked far more than he'd intended. If he lost Lara, he'd be nothing, have nothing. He flinched, but couldn't falter now. That would be cowardly. "It's true. I put a hit out on Adam."

"Why would you do that? Why?" Tight lines of disapproval bracketed her mouth, and her dark eyes flashed with emotion. Anger. Disappointment.

"I was jealous. My father wanted Adam to return to take over as Kokopelli."

"And that would be a bad thing?"

"I'd lose everything I've worked for."

"You think I'm so shallow I would turn from you during bad times?" A layer of hurt wove through the words, and they cut straight to the source of his tension with unerring accuracy.

A swift glance told him that while she wouldn't have walked away from him then, she might now. God, he'd been so blind. "I'd do anything to make it right, but it's too late. I can't cancel the contract."

"It's never too late," Lara said. "Tell me from the beginning. Everything."

So he told her everything, including his problem with the young woman who wanted to blackmail him, ending with the things he'd done regarding Adam. When he was done, she frowned.

"This will take some thought."

The load on his shoulders lightened with the problem shared. With his heart lighter, Justin nodded. "Perhaps we could think about it during our siesta?"

"No, you will sleep in the spare room until this is fixed." And Lara sailed from the room without looking back.

Justin swallowed audibly, resigned because he knew she wouldn't change her mind. His Lara was stubborn and determined when it came to right and wrong. Their marriage still amazed him. "Fuck." There had to be some way to fix this because he didn't care what happened to him now. All he wanted was to keep his wife at his side, to grow old with her. Perhaps he'd start by dealing with the troublesome woman who thought to blackmail him. Report her to the elders as he should have done straight away. He bore no guilt in turning her in because he'd never stepped out of line with her.

***

"SOMEONE IS WATCHING US again," Adam said as they checked into the hotel. "I've felt it off and on for the last month."

"It's you they're watching," Nate answered, scrawling his name on the registration card and handing over his credit card. He angled his hat a fraction as he turned to study the entranceway of the hotel. A young couple stood outside, the wife cradling her stomach with a protective hand as if she were pregnant. He was noticing a lot of pregnant women amongst their fans who traveled throughout the state to catch all the Stampede gigs. Must be something in the air because blooms covered the plants and trees this year, bringing vivid splashes of color to the town parks and gardens. Rosa would have said it was a good growing season. For the first time in a long while, the pain of Rosa's loss didn't strike him in the middle of his chest. Instead, he smiled inwardly because it was a good recollection. "The back of my neck only itches when I'm with you."

"It's gotta be a fan, then."

"Why haven't they come to you for an autograph? Tried to contact you? They're not behaving like a normal fan." Nate swung his overnight bag over his shoulder and walked to the elevator with Adam at his side.

"I don't know. It's not as if we can report this to the police. Whoever is watching hasn't done anything."

"We'll talk to the others, see if they've seen anyone or noticed anything unusual. It could be a reporter after a story."

Adam scowled. "Yeah, well that's worse. The last thing I

need is publicity."

"You should have thought of that before you made a move on me."

"Is that right?"

"It would have been more prudent."

"Who the hell wants prudent when they can have hot sex with the man of their dreams?"

"Sounds serious." Anxiety swept Nate. Adam shouldn't be with him. They shouldn't have checked into a hotel like this—not together when someone was following them around.

"Yeah, it's very serious." Adam waited until the doors closed behind them and prowled closer, backing him against the mirrored wall of the elevator. Adam grasped the brim of his hat and whisked it off. "Every time I look at you, all I can think about is stripping you naked."

A shiver raced through him at the intensity on Adam's face. He meant it. It wasn't just a line to get him into bed. Not that he intended to put up an argument. "Can we wait until we get to our room?" Nate took charge of his hat.

Adam's eyes narrowed as he stepped away. "You don't believe me. You think I'm playing you. Fuck, Nate. You're my friend. If this was just about sex I would have stayed away or at least told you upfront that all I wanted was a casual romp between the sheets. I would have demanded you let me fuck you properly instead of taking things slowly and waiting."

The flash of anger in Adam brought guilt. He had to stop doubting. "I'm sorry." He reached out to squeeze Adam's shoulder. "I—" The elevator car stopped and the doors opened. He let his hand drop to his side. Not their floor. A man and woman entered, and they stood in silence until the elevator stopped on their floor.

"I can't believe you'd think that little of me," Adam muttered.

"Do you think this is easy for me?" Aware of two room-service maids staring at them in curiosity, Nate held his tongue. He opened the door and stepped inside, holding it open for Adam. Only when he'd closed the doors, did he speak again. "You're my friend. Out of all the band members, you're the one I get on with best. Do you think I want to lose my job? That I don't wonder if we have a fight, I'll have to leave? Then there's the whole publicity thing. If our relationship comes out, it will cause trouble. The others know now."

"And you think they'll gossip?"

"No, all I'm saying is that an unguarded comment might cause problems."

"You're scared." Adam seemed pleased with his discovery.

"I'm not." But Nate knew Adam was right. This thing between them scared him silly. "Maybe," he amended cautiously.

"This isn't casual for me, Nate. I'm not trying to play you. You want a beer?"

Nate nodded and set down his bag. The room was a basic one with a queen-size bed, a wooden desk and one chair. A small en suite and a television rounded out the amenities. Nothing fancy, but at least it meant they'd have privacy without having to worry about someone disturbing them or overhearing their discussion. Adam handed him a beer, kicked off his boots and lounged back on the bed. He wriggled a fraction to get comfortable.

"There's something I need to talk to you about." Adam paused to sip his beer, and Nate unlaced his boots, kicking them under the desk before stretching out beside him on the bed.

"Sounds serious."

"I haven't told anyone this before."

Nate sent him a sharp look, and he couldn't stifle his swift grin. "Are you gonna tell me off for doubting you?"

"Nah, this is something else. A secret. You can't tell anyone."

"Maybe you shouldn't tell me then."

"Nate, I've told you. This relationship, what I feel for

you isn't casual. I know things have happened quickly and you don't trust me yet, but I want to put my faith in you. I want to show I trust you. This is one way of doing it. Besides, I could use some advice."

Alarm surged in Nate. "You're not sick, are you?"

"Of course not." Adam tugged up his T-shirt to bare his chest.

Nate gawked. He couldn't help it. The subtle tattoo he'd become used to glowed with color. He could have sworn it had been black ink. It wasn't now. "That's a Kokopelli."

Of course it was a Kokopelli, but...but how? When? Every time he'd broached the subject, Adam had avoided his questions, usually by jumping him and redirecting his thoughts. After a couple of times, Nate had gone straight to the sex stage because he figured Adam didn't want to discuss the tattoo. But that hadn't meant Nate's curiosity had faded.

"Yeah, it's Kokopelli."

"When...how...it wasn't like that this morning."

"This isn't a tattoo. It's a birthmark of sorts. It's hereditary." Adam paused to take another sip of beer and right his T-shirt. His throat felt tight, and fear rippled through him. The last thing he wanted was for Nate to think he was crazy. The Kokopelli had transformed from muted to vibrant colors during the course of the day, and he didn't know what this meant. "My family is directly descended from Kokopelli, and one male in each generation bears his powers. Despite being the younger brother, I inherited the powers in my generation, but my sexual orientation caused a problem." Adam cast an uncertain glance at Nate, continuing with his story when he received an encouraging nod. "When my father discovered I was gay, he kicked me out of the family home. My father and the village elders did a special ceremony in the hope the Kokopelli would fade from my chest. There was much celebration when the mark reappeared on my brother." The pain of rejection sliced through him in a vicious replay. He remembered packing his possessions and walking away while his family, friends and the villagers celebrated the arrival of a new Kokopelli.

"What powers does Kokopelli have? You're not messing with me, right?" Nate speared him with a sharp, dissecting look, as if he was trying to decide whether to believe or not. "You are. You're joking."

"No! Nate, you know I didn't have this done in a tattoo parlor. As for powers, Kokopelli brings fertility mainly, in crops and for women. Some people say he heralds in the seasons with his flute." Recently, he'd felt the low hum of energy pulsing through his body, an echo of the same force he recalled from when he'd borne the tattoo before. And pregnant women—every time he turned around he was seeing them or hearing of new pregnancies. It was both cool and scary at the same time. "Haven't you noticed all the flourishing plants everywhere? We stayed at this place when we did the gig here last year. Do you remember what the plants looked like then? All short and stunted. Do you remember Cade wondering why they bothered?"

"I have noticed the flowers this year." Nate frowned, and Adam thought he still looked unconvinced. "You play the flute?"

"Not anymore."

"Fertility?" Nate asked, his eyes narrowing. Adam could practically see Nate's mind ticking over and the questions forming. "You mean women get pregnant when you're around? I mean when the Kokopelli person is around? You don't do the deed yourself?"

"Fuck, no! Kokopelli passes on fertility with ritual words or flute playing. In the past, lots of children meant there were many hands to help with the work. Children made a man rich, so fertility was highly rated. These days, maybe not so much."

Adam hoped there wouldn't be too many unplanned pregnancies around the place. As long as he refrained from touching women, it shouldn't be a problem. *He hoped*. Hell, as if he didn't have enough to worry about. "Look, if you don't believe me, check out the plants at Colorado Springs when we hit town. After we've been there a few days, they'll seem healthier." Adam rolled his eyes. "It's freaky. Honest to God, I'm telling the truth."

"Okay, say I believe you." Nate set his beer aside, his frown still evident. "What does the appearance of the mark mean? Do you think something has happened to your brother?"

Adam swallowed, feeling marginally better for sharing, even though he had no answers. "I don't know. I should contact my father." He shrugged, the old pain and anger resurfacing.

"What about your brother? Could you call him?"

"Justin?" Adam shook his head. "My brother and I have nothing in common. I swear he hates me. He was pleased to see me leave. Nate, I don't know what to do."

Nate laughed suddenly. "At least I can't get pregnant, but maybe you should warn Cade."

"I can't go anywhere until we've finished the gigs Susan has booked for us. And we're working on the album."

"True." Nate nodded, his frown telling Adam he was considering all the possibilities. "You could always ring your father."

"No." That was the last thing he wanted to do. "I prefer a face-to-face meeting, get a sense of the nuances a bit better."

"And where's home?"

"New Mexico." He leaned back against the headboard, shifting a fraction before he found a comfortable spot. "By all accounts, my father and the Kokopelli before him used to spread their love around, but during the time I spent as Kokopelli, I never slept with anyone. That was part of the problem. Everyone started comparing notes and gossiping because I never touched any of the women."

"And the men?"

"I didn't touch them, either. The only time I had sex was when I went to the nearest city for a weekend."

"But you've had sex with a woman before?"

"Yeah, I figured I needed to be sure of my sexuality. It wasn't the same. I like being with a man better. What about you?"

Nate paused, and Adam cursed himself for the question. It wasn't cool being jealous of a dead woman.

"I don't think of the sex in terms of better," Nate said slowly. His gaze caught Adam's and, like a moth to light, he couldn't look away from the intensity in Nate's eyes. "It's the person who attracts me—their personality and the way we interact."

Adam's heart started to pound, his cock going instantly hard. "Maybe we could talk more later."

A sexy smile bloomed, making Nate's eyes sparkle. "I couldn't agree more." He took Adam's beer bottle from him.

"Take off your shirt."

Adam shivered at the expression on Nate's face, the way he took charge. Eagerly, he yanked his T-shirt over his head, shivering again at the hot intent in Nate's eyes. He swallowed, his hands going to the fly of his jeans.

"No, just your shirt for now."

"Jeans aren't comfortable with a hard-on."

Nate's brows rose, a smile playing at the corner of his lips. "That right?"

"Payback can be a bitch."

"But fun."

Adam nodded, returning to the mattress, a little wary now as he wondered exactly what Nate intended to do with him.

"You weren't kidding about the tat, were you?" Nate traced the edges of his Kokopelli. The faint drag of his finger shot sensation straight to Adam's balls, and he groaned. "Sensitive?"

"Yeah. I don't remember it being like this. And the tat was never so bright before."

Nate laughed. "Maybe you're taking Kokopelli into the next century."

"Yeah, well, I won't be having any kids to pass the baton to the next generation. That's why this is so weird."

Nate leaned over him and replaced his finger with his tongue. Adam groaned, closing his eyes to better concentrate on the sensations. Nate's warm tongue. The faint nibble of teeth. The rasp of his whiskers. The sensations washed over him, and he floated in the pleasure. Nate's scent filled his every breath, the soft sound of his breathing and the faint tick of the clock sitting on the table beside him the only things he could hear.

Nate stroked his chest and moved his attention to one nipple, worrying it until it rose to a taut nub. His large hands mapped Adam's body, alternately stroking and pinching until Adam moaned with pleasure and desperately wanted more.

"More." He tried not to sound too desperate.

Nate just laughed and lightly cupped his swollen erection. Adam groaned, the slight friction of Nate's hand making him see stars. He wasn't gonna last long at this rate.

"Let's get you out of these jeans." Nate maneuvered the zipper over his cock and peeled the denim away.

The release of pressure was a relief, and he sighed when Nate pulled his underwear down and lifted his cock free. Seconds later, the gentle suction of Nate's mouth fuelled his need.

"Damn, Nate. Are you trying to kill me?"

Nate hummed around his cock, watching his face the entire time. With a distinct twinkle in his dark eyes, he pushed one of his fingers into his mouth, sliding it alongside Adam's cock until it was wet. While he continued the lazy stroke of his tongue and the easy suction, he rubbed his finger over the nerve-rich opening of Adam's anus.

"Nate," Adam whispered, canting his hips upward in a silent demand for more. With a steady gaze, Nate watched him. His eyes glittered with heat, his lean cheeks hollowing when he sucked. A surge of desire hit him, his balls tingling enough to make him gasp. "It's time, right?" Adam gripped Nate's shoulders, suddenly anxious. He wanted Nate to claim him properly. Surely Nate trusted him fully by now? It was time to take the next step in their relationship. "There's lube and condoms in the side pocket of my bag."

Nate released his cock with a loud smacking sound. "Guess I'd better get them, then."

Relief struck Adam. Need grabbed him by the throat, and even though Nate no longer touched him, his entire body pulsed, his skin super sensitive, his balls hard and aching. He heard the zip of his bag whine when Nate went looking for the lube and condoms. Lifting his head, he watched Nate discard his clothes. Like a striptease, beautiful muscles honed by running and lugging the band's equipment were revealed. Sculpted. Sexy. His to touch. His mouth watered as Nate started to undo his fly. Slowly, his lover peeled off the denim and stepped from his jeans, leaving the black boxer-briefs that did nothing to conceal his erection.

Adam rolled toward the edge of the bed, a hungry moan escaping him. "Let me touch you. Please."

With hooded eyes, Nate approached the bed. Adam raised his head a fraction until his mouth was level with Nate's groin. He leaned closer and exhaled.

A noticeable tremor went through Nate. "Are you going to touch?"

"You've made me wait." Adam wanted to tease him, wanted to watch his expression, see the need rise to his face.

Nate placed the lube and several condoms on the bed stand. "I don't do casual."

God, he loved this side of Nate—the strong, silent man who liked things done his way. With anticipation humming through him, Adam spread his thighs and waited. As he watched, Nate stripped off the boxer-briefs, letting his cock spill free. With his gaze on Adam, he stroked himself, hand fisting around his cock and a faint smile playing around his lips.

SHELLEY MUNRO

"Not fair," Adam protested.

"Just wanted to make sure I had your attention. Besides, you didn't want to touch me."

"Not true. Come over here. I'd be happy to touch you."

Nate chuckled and grabbed a condom. He ripped the foil packaging open with his teeth and competently rolled it on. He picked up the lube next and squirted a dollop into his hand. Adam's breath caught and released on a moan as Nate rubbed the lube on his cock instead of on him. His condom-covered cock glistened in the light.

"There's no rush," Nate soothed, although his voice held amusement as he worked his cock again.

Adam groaned, his dick aching for handling. He grasped it and pumped firmly. "Don't you think we've gone slowly for long enough? I think a little speed would be a good thing."

"Hands above your head," Nate ordered. "No touching." The no-nonsense tone held determination.

Adam forced a scowl when what he really wanted to do was grin. He peeled his fingers away from his swollen flesh, anticipation flooding him as he basked under Nate's attention.

"How do you want to do this?"

Adam wanted to see the passion racing across Nate's face, see the moment his lover came, and most of all, he

192

wanted to be able to touch him easily, to kiss those sexy lips and feel the rasp of beard against his skin. "I want to watch your face."

"We can do that."

The mattress depressed with Nate's weight, and another shiver worked down his spine. He wanted this so much, could hardly believe they'd finally made it this far where Nate was not only willing to have sex with him, but was taking charge, taking responsibility for their pleasure.

"Dammit, touch me. I can't wait any longer."

Nate ran a finger the length of Adam's shaft. His cock bucked at the barely there touch, his throat working in a swallow as he fought to maintain his control. He would not come like an overexcited teenager.

"But I like watching your reactions. When you're playing music and you're up on stage, I can't always read you. When we're alone together, it's easy. I know that you're silently cursing me for teasing you, yet you haven't complained much."

"I'm working up to complaints," Adam said gruffly. "Believe me, they're coming."

"Can't have that." Nate started to caress him, gripping his dick more firmly with one hand.

As Adam watched, a drop of pre-come formed at his slit. Nate moved closer, and Adam beseeched him silently, his breath easing out with relief when a finger slid across his hole.

"Yes," he hissed.

"Impatient." Nate's husky chuckle slammed hunger through Adam. He wriggled, trying to impale himself on Nate's finger.

"Need you."

"Okay," Nate said.

Adam watched him pick up the bottle of lube with a sense of excitement. Nate squeezed a dollop onto his palm, and he started to work him, to stretch him, slick fingers sliding inside his hole. A hiss of pleasure escaped Adam, euphoria filling him with every gliding stroke of Nate's blunt finger. This had been worth the wait. Gradually, Nate increased the number of fingers, stretching him to a point where discomfort edged into the equation. Adam dragged in a quick breath and blew it out, knowing this would pass soon. He consciously relaxed, and the pleasure returned.

"Now, Nate. Take me now. Please." To his relief, Nate shifted over him. He moved tentatively at first, allowing Adam to adjust to his possession, get past the initial burn. Then he moved faster, thrust harder and sank in to the hilt. Nate pounded his ass, exerting a physical claim, and Adam loved every moment. Their lips met in an urgent kiss, a clash of lips and teeth. Nate's flavor and scent rushed his senses, filled and surrounded him. His fingers grazed the Kokopelli tattoo, an echo of Nate's touch making his cock buck.

"Aw, damn." Adam clutched Nate's shoulders and held tight, enjoying the ride, the sense of closeness. He didn't remember the tattoo being so sensitive, a lover's touch bringing so much heat, so much pleasure. Their sweat-slicked torsos stuck together. Adam didn't care. He panted through another stroke, gritting his teeth to stop himself from coming too soon.

"You okay? Want me to stop?"

"No, don't stop," Adam ordered urgently. It worked, because Nate continued to push deep, retreating and invading until Adam felt well and truly claimed. Pleasure started to grow, nerve endings firing like electrical circuits. Fully seated, Nate paused to kiss Adam, their lips brushing, eyes smoldering as they tasted each other and their breath blended.

"I knew this would feel good," Adam said, his hands gripping Nate's shoulders and holding tight. "I could get used to this." The guttural admission echoed between them, and Adam knew they'd been right to delay the physical intimacies in their relationship. The wait had made their first time something he'd always remember.

When Nate didn't say anything, a wave of fear hit him. Were his feelings one-sided and not returned by Nate? He swallowed, his gaze on his lover's strong jawline. Maybe he needed to give Nate more time to get used to the idea of a serious relationship and life after Rosa. If there was one thing Adam knew, it was that he didn't want to do casual anymore.

Nate rubbed his lips against his, caught Adam's bottom lip and nipped it. "It can feel better," he promised, and he started to move again with strong, even strokes while one of his hands gripped Adam's cock to combine the sweet burn in his ass with the dragging friction on his shaft. "How's that feel?"

"Good." An understatement. It felt more than good, especially when Nate angled his strokes and nailed his gland. Adam wrapped his arms around his lover, kissed the heavy slab of muscle on his chest and gave him a hint of teeth.

"Yeah." Nate quickened his strokes, sliding deep, going faster. He reached for one of Adam's hands, entwining their fingers. The intimate connection made Adam's heart stall before it jumped into a racy beat. This was what he wanted for his future.

The pleasant burn settled in his balls, drawing them tight until he thought he'd explode any second. A hard stroke caught his prostate again. Aw, hell. A groan slipped free as the tension snapped and semen pulsed from his cock. A hungry growl squeezed from Nate as he tunneled in and out of Adam's ass. Then he stilled.

"Fuck, that feels awesome." Nate's face contorted as he climaxed, his cock jerking so hard Adam could feel it. He fell forward, leaning heavily on Adam.

Adam didn't mind. He smiled and clung, uncaring of the sticky residue coating his stomach. Nate had definitely been worth the wait.

"I suppose you want me to move," Nate grumbled finally.

"Breathing's good," Adam agreed.

"Huh. I thought it was highly overrated." But Nate levered away and pulled from him. He wandered away to the en suite and, soon, Adam heard the shower. Not a bad idea, he thought, despite his disappointment that Nate hadn't returned to their bed. They did some of their best work in the shower.

When he entered the en suite, Nate was already standing under the warm water and rubbing a bar of soap over his chest. Adam opened the door and slipped in beside him, briskly washing his chest.

"I was gonna bring you a cloth to clean up."

"It's no hardship jumping into the shower with you."

Weak. The truth was, even though they were together now, Adam worried about their future. At least Nate hadn't reacted badly when he'd told him about Kokopelli.

"Turn around, and I'll do your back."

Silently, Adam turned and braced his hands against the tiled wall of the shower. Hell, he didn't even know what the return of his tattoo meant. It worried him because with the return of the tattoo came responsibility to his family and the villagers. It would mean he'd have to return home, and Adam didn't want to do that when the band was starting to gain traction. His music was too important to him. No, giving up music wasn't an option.

CHAPTER TEN

THE BAND SOUNDED GREAT, Nate thought as they wound up another song. They were back in the Denver studio belonging to Susan's friend, working on their album. As always, Nate's attention returned to Adam. Dressed in an old T-shirt and faded jeans, he threw his heart into the song. He loved music, and it showed.

Buoyed by the music, Nate's mind drifted back to the previous evening and the big revelation about Adam and his family. It was the first time Adam had even mentioned his family. Nate knew more about J.T., Cade and Morgan's families than he knew about Adam's. A swift glance at his watch showed he had enough time to run to the library to do some research. He wanted to know exactly what they were dealing with. Nate frowned. It was possible Adam hadn't told him everything. Yeah, research sounded like a plan. The band didn't need him for another couple of hours.

The studio was in the center of town and, as it happened, not far from the library. Nate pushed through the double doors and stepped onto the pavement. The wind stirred his hair, the scent of coffee tempting him to stop at the café on the corner to grab a cup to go.

Weird. The usual prickling sensation he experienced when he was with Adam wasn't present. Nate glanced over his shoulder and also scanned the street in front of him before he entered the library.

The legend of Kokopelli—the facts were much as Adam had told him, except nothing he found online or in research books indicated the presence of a real person connected to the legend. But he'd seen the tattoo himself, and he knew it hadn't been there when they first became closer. The tattoo hadn't been there when they'd jumped into the hot tub together. Adam obviously believed the myth.

Nate thought back over the last few months. Some weird shit had happened, that was for sure. Adam's confession about being Kokopelli was the last item in a long line of bizarre occurrences. Nate clicked on a link to read yet another web page about Kokopelli.

Who had become Kokopelli after Adam had left?

Adam had said it was his brother, but he didn't know for sure. Nate stared at the computer screen, then did a search for Justin James. Several web pages came up. Nate scanned the headings, finally choosing one. New Mexico. Adam's family lived in New Mexico. And there had been a recent marriage. Nate couldn't see a family resemblance, but that didn't mean anything.

Nate left the library to the shrill sound of a police siren. He turned right to head to the studio, slowing when the police pulled up outside. His gut lurched, sudden fear jumping through him.

But the cops didn't enter the studio building. Instead, they went into the building next door. A woman talked to them, and they disappeared from sight.

"What's goin' on?" an elderly woman asked.

Yeah, exactly what he wanted to know.

A middle-aged woman stared in the direction the cops had taken. "They had reports of a Peeping Tom on the roof. One of the residents, a nice young woman, told me she saw a man on the roof last week. Maybe she saw him again." She shook her head, setting her auburn curls bouncing. "A terrible business."

Nate checked his watch again and decided to hang around. They'd visited the studio last week for a few hours.

A coincidence?

Another police car pulled up, and this time the cops moved at a brisk pace. A shot fired. Nate's head snapped in the direction of the sound. The elderly woman gasped and darted into the nearest shop. The street cleared magically, and Nate pressed against the brick wall of the building. Another shot fired, but he didn't hear a third. Thirty minutes later, the police exited the building and drove away.

Surely they wouldn't leave if a gunman remained on the loose? Nate entered the studio building, nodded at the doorman and arrived in time to hear the end of the final song.

"How were we?" Cade asked.

"Good as always," Nate said, meaning it. He was proud of them. "I'll go and get the van. There was some trouble outside, and I'd prefer to pick you guys up at the door."

Adam jogged over to his side and, for a second, Nate thought he was gonna embrace him and land a kiss smack on his lips with everyone looking. Susan would really approve of that. "What sort of trouble? I'll come with you."

"No," Nate said. "Gunfire type of trouble. The cops have gone, but I don't want to take any chances. I'll pull up right outside when you come out. Wait for the doorman to tell you I've arrived before you come outside." He left before the others could get in any questions.

When he got to the van, he checked the vicinity before unlocking it and climbing behind the wheel. He switched on the radio and caught a newsflash about the gunman.

"Police are no closer to learning the identity of the lone gunman who fired shots at them earlier this afternoon," the female newsreader said. "Police were called to the Regent Building after reports of a Peeping Tom. Several inhabitants of the luxury apartment block complained to the police of a stranger loitering in the vicinity and spying through windows. A spokesman from the police department said the man fired on the attending officers when they hailed him, and he disappeared, evading capture. Police say they think they shot the man when they returned fire. Anyone with knowledge of the man or who suspects they know his identity should contact their local police station."

That didn't sound good. Nate started the van and drove around the block, pulling up in the loading zone in front of the studio building. He climbed from the van and opened the side door before gesturing at the doorman. The band emerged, too slowly for Nate's liking.

"Move it," he snapped.

"What's wrong with you?" Adam asked, shoving

Morgan aside to take possession of the passenger seat.

"The gunman is still on the loose."

"So?" J.T. said. "It's got nothing to do with us."

Nate slammed the side door shut once they were all inside and stomped around to the driver's side. "You don't think it's weird that Adam and I are shot at while we're running, our motel is broken into, and now there's a gunman loitering near the studio where the band is recording?"

There was a moment of startled silence.

"Coincidence," Adam said.

"I don't know. Nate is right." Morgan studied Adam as if he were a freak at a sideshow. "Put together it does sound suspicious. Adam, who the hell have you pissed off?"

"No one." Adam shot Nate a warning look.

Nate ignored the warning. "I think someone is out to get Adam." He voiced the fear bubbling inside him. "Every time we're outside, the back of my neck prickles as if someone is watching. Haven't any of you noticed?"

Morgan grunted. "I have, but I didn't say anything. Come to think of it, it's always when we're with Adam. When I'm alone or with one of the others, I haven't noticed anything out of the ordinary."

"Why would someone want to hurt Adam?" Cade asked. "Everyone likes him."

"Maybe it's an overzealous fan," J.T. said.

"That doesn't make sense. A fan like that normally writes letters and stalks openly. This is more behind-the-scenes stuff. More dangerous." Nate pulled into the rush hour traffic and headed for their motel. "I think we need to shake up our routine a little and do things at random times. Wear hats when we go out and dress in a similar manner. We're all about the same height. At a distance, it would be difficult for someone to tell us apart."

"But that would put everyone in danger," Adam protested.

"Ah, so you admit Nate isn't talking through a hole in his head." Cade leaned forward between the seats. "You think there's an element of truth in what he's saying."

"I— Yeah, maybe," Adam said, shrugging in a casual manner belying the seriousness of the problem. "Once we're finished with the tracks we're putting down, Nate and I are going to visit my family for a few days, anyway. By then the cops should have caught the gunman and everything will return to normal."

"And what if it's not okay?" Morgan asked. "What if this guy is after you? Shouldn't you tell the cops?"

"We've already reported the shooting and the break-ins," Adam said. "There's not much more we can do."

"I agree we should take care with security," Cade said. "That's not stupid. Even if we tell the cops our suspicions, Adam's right in saying there's not much they can do. We'll have to play it by ear and watch out for each other. Think, have you pissed anyone off lately?"

"No one!" Adam said.

"Past lovers?" Nate asked.

"Good one, Nate." Morgan sniggered. "That's a good way of worming info out of him about his love life."

"Nate knows about my past," Adam said. "We don't have any secrets."

"You kept secrets from us," J.T. reminded them. "And we're your best friends."

Nate kept driving, not wanting to add anything else. It was Adam's place to tell them about Kokopelli if he wanted to. He'd done his job and made them aware of security. At this stage, there was nothing more they could do.

"Have you reached the assassin to cancel the contract?" Lara asked.

Justin winced, resenting the reminder of his failure to put right his wrongs. "I've tried. The contact number I have goes to voice mail. I've left several messages, and I've tried the email contact."

Lara set a mug of coffee in front of him, a frown on her pretty face. Justin hated seeing the scowl and would do anything to make it disappear. He'd thought he'd been happy before. He'd been wrong. Happiness was holding Lara. Happiness was spending time with his wife, making love with her. Never had he experienced such a connection before and he thanked the gods every day for bringing her into his life. Thank goodness she'd relaxed her rule about sleeping in the same room.

"You should contact your brother. Tell him what you've done."

Justin realized his mouth was agape and shut it firmly. "I..." He trailed off, closing his eyes to marshal his thoughts. He knew Lara was right, knew it with every ounce of his soul, but he couldn't. Lara didn't know how hard he'd tried to shoot his brother. He would have done it, gone through with the murder if the other park visitors hadn't interrupted him. But that was then. He'd changed in such a short time. He didn't want Adam dead now. While he didn't want to give up the prestige of being Kokopelli, he wanted to do a good job now instead of exploiting people in exchange for his benevolence. Hell, listen to him. Lara had changed him. Six months ago, he'd never imagined being in this position.

"My brother and I parted on bad terms. I'm not sure he'll agree to speak with me."

"We will visit him in person," Lara said firmly. She smiled then, a mysterious curve to her lips. Her hand slid over her belly, and in that instant Justin knew. His heart beat in three hard pumps of anticipation.

"Are you—?"

"We're going to have a baby, Justin."

Justin sprang off his chair and dragged her into his arms, squeezing her in his exuberance. A father. He couldn't believe it had happened so soon. Oh, he'd hoped, but he'd expected it to take time. He was going to be a father.

Lara was beaming when she pulled back. So pretty. Her cheeks glowed, and he'd never loved her more. "We need to tell your brother. Do you know where he is now?"

"In Wyoming, I think. That's where he was the last time I checked. He has a band called Stampede. If we can find the band, where they're playing, then we should find Adam."

"I will do a search on the Internet as soon as we finish our dinner."

"All right. You find Adam, and I'll go to visit him."

"No," Lara said. "I'm going to visit your brother with you."

"No!" Justin said, fear rippling through him. "No. It's dangerous. I don't want anything to happen to you, to the baby."

"Justin, you put a contract out on your brother. At some point, you wanted your brother dead. The least we can do is to warn him." Her small chin lifted in determination, and Justin sighed. He knew what that look meant. Sometimes Lara would discuss things, let him persuade her from her course of action, but this was her stubborn look. The look that told him she'd dig her toes in and refuse to divert her path. She wanted him to talk to Adam and intended to witness their meeting.

Justin thought about the assassin lurking in the shadows, his gun—the man's preferred method of execution—trained on Adam, trailing his every move. What if he shot Lara by mistake while they were with Adam?

Oh, hell.

Justin forced a smile and nodded, even though acute fear lay in the pit of his stomach. He'd die if anything happened to Lara. Maybe he could contact the police, tell them about the assassin and the man's target. No! No, he couldn't do that. They'd ask questions, want to know how he knew.

"What? What are you thinking?"

"Maybe I could ring the police and leave them an

anonymous tip?"

"Wouldn't that cause trouble if the assassin learned you'd passed on information about him?" Lara sounded worried, and he realized how lucky he was that she was still talking to him, still believed in him despite the bad things he'd done in his life. Meeting Lara and marrying her was a second chance, and he didn't intend to screw it up.

"Yes, probably. If he found out. How would he find out?"

"The man isn't stupid. Didn't you say he's been doing this for a long time? He hasn't survived by making mistakes."

Once again, Lara made sense. Justin recalled the weeks it had taken him to even contact the assassin, and all the hurdles he'd had to leap to organize the hit in the first place. Lara was right. An anonymous tip would likely do more harm than good.

"All right. Find Adam for me, and we'll go and see him together." And they'd discuss the topic of Kokopelli, because it was obvious Justin was no longer the chosen one. Transference out of the family line had occurred on rare occasions in the past, but the powers had always returned to the James's line. No one else in the village had come forward, which meant...

Hell, he didn't know what it meant. That's why he

needed to discuss the situation with Adam. Better his brother than their father. Their father always expected so much of them, the burden becoming too much at times. Was it any wonder both he and his brother had rebelled in their own way?

THE NEXT MORNING, NATE left their motel room and scanned his surroundings, searching for anything out of the ordinary. To his right, a profusion of flowers in the garden beds offered a burst of color against a plain brick wall. The buzz of hard-working bees vibrated through the air, the insects flitting from bloom to bloom. A row of flowering trees, branches covered with furled buds and numerous leaves, swayed in the gentle breeze. A dog lifted its leg, relieving itself on one of the trunks. When nothing suspicious grabbed Nate's attention and the itchiness at the back of his neck didn't arrive as usual, he gestured for the guys to exit.

"I feel as if I'm walking around with a cross painted on my back," Cade grumbled as they piled into the van to head out for another day at the studio.

J.T. snorted. "I know what you mean. I keep looking over my shoulder. An old lady scared the crap out of me in the café this morning."

"He had to go and change his underwear," Cade said with a chuckle.

Morgan scowled. "I still think we should go to the police."

"And tell them what?" Adam snapped.

Nate squeezed his shoulder in silent sympathy and urged him inside the van. This wasn't easy on any of them, and Adam in particular.

"I'm sitting in the front with you," Adam said, shrugging off Nate's hand and stomping around the front of the van before Nate could stop him.

Biting his tongue, Nate climbed behind the wheel and started the van. He wanted to shout at Adam and tell him not to be such a stupid fool. It would kill him if something happened to Adam. Rosa's death had almost done him in. He couldn't lose Adam as well, not now that he'd finally found him to love.

"Fuck!" Nate jammed on the brakes.

"What's wrong?" Morgan demanded from the rear.

"Did you see something?" Cade asked.

"No, it was private," Nate answered, still stunned at his sudden realization. He loved Adam. When the hell had that happened? Yeah, he enjoyed spending time with Adam, he enjoyed the sex, but love... After Rosa, he'd decided he'd never put himself in that position again.

"Did you and Adam have a domestic?" J.T. asked.

Adam snapped, "No, we did not!"

"Oh, it speaks," Cade mocked.

"Knock it off," Adam ordered. "I have a family problem I have to deal with, and I can't think with you rattling your jaws."

"You have a family?" J.T. teased. "I thought they found you in a cabbage patch somewhere."

"That was your parents," Adam shot back.

Morgan frowned. "So why don't you ever talk about your family?"

"We're not close. I told you the other day I had a difficult relationship with my father." Adam clicked his seatbelt into place.

"I thought it must be something like that," Cade said. "I remember when we first met in the pub in that small hick town. You didn't say much."

"But I could sing and play the sax ten times better than any of you, so you decided to keep me around," Adam said in a smug voice.

Nate hid a smirk, loving the interplay between the men. They'd made him welcome from the start, drawn him into their family and helped him fill the huge gap in his life left by Rosa's death. He pulled up at a set of traffic lights and listened to the good-natured insults that bounced from one man to the next while he waited for the signal to turn green.

"Light's changed," Adam prompted him, placing his hand on Nate's knee.

Nate sucked in a hasty breath, worried about the others seeing. "I see it." Although he knew their relationship was no longer a secret, he couldn't help glancing in the rearview mirror to see if the others had noticed the intimacy.

"Hands off the driver," Cade piped up. "He needs to concentrate on driving."

"I'm concentrating," Nate said, accelerating smoothly into the intersection.

"Holy fuck! Watch out," Adam shouted.

The words had scarcely left his mouth when a gray sedan barreled into the passenger side of the van. Nate spun the wheel, but too late. The impact sent the van skidding into the path of a blue SUV. Horns tooted. Brakes shrieked. Nate cursed, flung forward against his seatbelt by the impact of the second vehicle. The front airbags exploded, engulfing him when gravity flung him forward. Nate gasped for air, struggling against the airbag. His leg. He couldn't move his damn leg. And blood. He could feel the wet seep of blood running down his calf. Damn airbag.

He couldn't see a thing. The van jolted to a sharp halt, then there was silence, apart from a loud moan coming from the rear of the van. Nate shoved the airbag out of the way, cataloging the ache in his right shoulder in the back of his mind, trying to see his leg. He tried to lift it. The slash of pain forced a groan from him.

"Nate? You okay?" Adam sounded frantic.

"Yeah. Yeah, I'm fine." Or he would be when he could get out of this tin can. "Everyone okay in the back?"

"Think so," Cade said.

"What the fuck happened?" Morgan asked.

A horn droned in the background. Outside, people shouted. Nate could see smoke coming from the gray vehicle, smell gasoline. They needed to get out right now.

"Everybody out," he ordered. "We need to get out of the van."

"My door won't open," Adam said.

A siren sounded in the distance, coming closer and closer.

"My door won't open, either," Nate said, fear starting to rise inside him because of the amount of smoke rising from the sedan.

"Try the side door. Morgan? Cade?"

One of the guys at the back grunted, pounded on the door with his fist once.

215

"It won't damn well budge." Cade sounded frustrated, a thread of alarm splintering his voice. Nate understood exactly how he felt. The building smoke obscured his vision through the windshield as he struggled with the airbag and the seatbelt.

A masculine shout came from outside, metal screeched and the side door wrenched open with a sickening crunch.

"You guys okay?" a man asked.

"Mostly," Cade answered for them all.

"You need to get out," the man said tersely. "I don't like the amount of smoke." As he spoke, he reached for Cade to help him out of the van.

"Adam, can you crawl out the back?" Nate didn't like the look of the blood trickling down Adam's face. "Go on," he said, couching it as an order. "You first. You're bleeding."

"And you're right after me. Right?"

"Don't you worry. I'll be on your heels." *If he could move.* His left leg seemed to be stuck somehow, and he could still feel the slickness of blood on his lower leg. He willed Adam to leave the van and gave a soft sigh of relief when his lover finally started to move.

Adam cast a last, worried glance at Nate, then crawled past him, concentrating on dragging his aching body over the console and into the back of the van. Every bone in

Adam's body ached, and his head thumped in time. A drop of blood plopped on his arm, drawing his attention. He shuddered and hurriedly looked away, focusing instead on the open door and the stranger standing there ready to help him out.

The driver in the gray car had purposely rammed them. Adam had seen it with his own eyes, his gaze connecting with the driver's just before the impact. His hands clenched around the top of a seat. Yeah, there were a few things he'd like to say to that crazy son-of-a-bitch. Like what the hell was his problem? Nate hadn't done anything wrong. He hadn't committed any traffic offenses.

Finally, strong arms grasped Adam firmly and took some of the strain, yanking him from the van. Once on his feet, he wobbled slightly, feeling lightheaded.

"Whoa! Man, you okay?" a man asked.

Adam fought past the woozy sensation. "Can you help Nate? He's the last one."

A cop hurried past and peered inside the van. A second cop took Adam by the arm and drew him away, toward the other band members.

"What the fuck happened?" Morgan asked. "I'm sure Nate didn't do anything wrong. He had a green light."

Adam stared over J.T.'s shoulder at the wrecked gray vehicle. A man lay on the ground near the car, a bystander working on him. Probably a doctor. "The guy in the gray car aimed his vehicle at the van. I saw him, saw the look on his face." Before he'd even finished the words, Adam strode toward the man and the crumpled gray sedan. He wanted to talk to him, intended to talk to him and ask why.

"Stand back," a cop ordered.

"No. I need to talk to this guy." He ignored the cop, intent on his goal.

"Let him talk," the man lying on the ground rasped out.

"Just a moment," the cop agreed.

Adam stumbled to the man's side and crouched down. "Who are you? Why did you smash into us?" He scanned the man's grizzled face with not a jot of recognition. Bulky bandages, now blood-splattered, covered his upper right arm, and the doctor pushed a heavy cotton pad against his chest. Blood turned his white T-shirt red.

"You...you ruined my life," the man gritted out.

"Me? I don't even know you."

The man said something, his voice so weak Adam couldn't hear. Adam leaned forward to hear. "You have the devil's own luck. I've tried to shoot you four times. Line you up and you'd move, someone would get in the way. Someone called the cops on me." He paused to gasp, his breath coming in a bubbling wheeze.

The wail of a siren told Adam he'd need to hurry because

it was coming closer and closer. The man didn't look good. Even if he hadn't guessed the man wasn't far from death, a quick glance at the cop's face would have clued him in. "Why the fuck are you trying to shoot me? I don't even know you."

"Job. Paid." The words were scarcely more than strained whispers.

"Someone paid you to shoot me," Adam snarled, his voice rising in anger. What the fuck had he done to deserve that? He smiled at children, opened the door for old ladies. "Who? Who the fuck would do that?"

The man made another of those bubbling sounds deep in his chest, coughed weakly, and Adam saw blood at the corners of his lips. His face was deadly pale, but his eyes glittered without repentance.

"Who?" Adam leaned even closer, ignoring the jagged pain in his head.

"J...Just." The man's face went slack, and his head dropped to the side.

"No!" Adam howled. "Just what?"

An ambulance pulled up, and medics jumped out. One grabbed Adam while the other consulted with the doctor and started to work on the stranger.

Beneath his T-shirt, the Kokopelli tattoo pulsed, and he focused on that heat, drawing from it. Someone wanted him dead. The man had tried to kill him, not once but several times. All the accidents, the close calls—Nate had been right. He didn't get it.

Did. Not. Get. It.

A cop walked over. "We need a medic at the van. The driver's leg is trapped. We want you to take a look before we cut him out."

Adam's head lifted sharply. "Nate? Nate's trapped?" Judging by the smoke coming from the engine, it looked as if it might catch on fire. A fire truck sped into the intersection and within seconds the firemen were grabbing equipment and examining the scene. It didn't help the fear that exploded inside him. Nate was injured, yet he'd never said a thing. God, he couldn't lose Nate. Nate meant everything to him.

"Don't move," the medic ordered. "Let me check your head."

"But Nate—" Two tears ran down his face, and his turmoil showed in his voice. "Nate is—"

"It's okay," Morgan said, his hand briefly squeezing Adam's shoulder. "They cut him out. He's safe."

"Nate's okay, Adam. His leg is cut badly, but he's not gonna die. He's okay," J.T. added.

The fight went out of Adam, and he nodded weakly. "Someone better ring Susan at the studio."

"Cade's already doing that."

"Are you almost done? I need to check on Nate," Adam told the medic. Everything would be better if he could just see Nate.

"Do you have a headache?"

"A bit," Adam conceded, minimizing the pain throbbing through his head.

"Any sharp pains?"

Adam hesitated, and the medic's mouth firmed. "You need to go to the hospital to get your head checked out."

"Nate's going to the hospital too," Morgan said quickly.

Adam nodded and wished he hadn't. He winced. The medic, who had been watching him, frowned and hustled him into the ambulance.

"We'll find a cab and follow you to the hospital," Cade said.

"Thanks." Man, his head hurt. He gingerly prodded the bump on the side of his skull and his fingers came away bloody. Shit, he hated the sight of blood. Hurriedly, he looked away, but the vision of red had seared across his retinas.

A thump beside him made him jerk his head. A pained groan escaped at the resulting agony.

"You okay?" Nate asked in an anxious voice. He leaned heavily on a medic, and blood covered his jeans. The medic had hacked off the left leg of his jeans, cutting it away from his leg, and fresh blood glistened on the padding covering the wound. It was too much for Adam. His eyes rolled back, and that was the last he remembered.

"Medic!" Nate snapped. "Something's wrong with him."

"He's probably fainted," Cade said from outside. "He's not very good with blood."

A medic brushed past him to check Adam. "Breathing and color is good. Pulse feels normal. We'll get him checked out at the emergency room, but I think your friend is right. He's fainted."

Fainted. What a girl! Nate smiled despite the pain throbbing along his left leg. He wouldn't let Adam forget this in a hurry.

CHAPTER ELEVEN

AFTER A THREE-HOUR WAIT, they released both of them from the hospital, although under protest. Adam couldn't wait to get back to the motel. He wanted to go to bed with Nate beside him and sleep for as long as it took before this nightmare ended.

He'd thought and thought about the man's words, the fact that someone had paid hard cash in order to see him dead. No matter how much Adam didn't want to believe it, "just" could be his brother, Justin. That would make sense, apart from the fact he hadn't seen him for years. The more he considered the idea, the more ludicrous it seemed, yet the Kokopelli tattoo had returned to his chest. What was up with that?

His head snapped up, his eyes widening as it hit him.

What if Justin had lost his powers? If Kokopelli died, the powers passed automatically to the closest relative. Fuck, what if his brother had died and no one had seen fit to inform him? He hadn't considered that earlier. Pain sliced through him, and it wasn't entirely due to the bump on his head. Despite the gap between him and his father, the open disapproval of his chosen lifestyle, he still thought of them as his family. A part of him had thought they would change their minds about disowning him.

What if they had another candidate in mind for Kokopelli and he stood in the way? If he and Justin were both dead, then would the Kokopelli powers pass to their oldest cousin? Would his father and the other elders take things to that extreme to protect the traditional ways?

He needed to go home. That much was obvious.

"I need to go home," he said out loud.

"Where's home?" Morgan asked.

"A small dot on the map in New Mexico. I doubt you've heard of Gainesville, because there's not much there. It's a two-hour drive to the nearest town."

"Why is it so important for you to go home now? Can't it wait?" Cade asked.

The cab pulled up in front of the motel. They climbed out, and Morgan paid the driver. J.T. arrived not long after with Susan and Nate.

"Quick meeting," Susan said.

They all ended up in Adam and Nate's room. Ignoring his headache, Adam helped Nate onto the bed and took the crutches, placing them beside the bed for Nate to grab when he needed them.

"I've canceled your gigs for the next week to give you all time to recover. The doctor said Adam needed a week, that his headaches might take a while to subside. You've made good progress with putting down the tracks for the new album, so I'm not worried about that. Is there anything else I need to take care of? Anything else I can do to help before I head out of town?"

"Thanks, Susan," Cade said for all of them. "I think we could all do with some downtime after today."

"Thanks." Adam seconded Cade. He knew they'd lose money by canceling the gigs for the next week, but they could do with a break. And it would give him time to visit home.

Susan left before anyone spoke.

"Can I have a glass of water?" Nate asked. "It's time to take my pills."

"I'll get it," Morgan said.

Adam studied Nate, taking in the pale face and tight lips. He edged closer, needing to touch Nate, to reassure himself his lover was okay. He reached for Nate's hand, his heart thudding when Nate glanced at him and shifted his hand to clasp his. Their fingers laced together, and some of Adam's panic faded.

Morgan returned, arched his brows a little when he noticed their linked hands, but he handed over the water to Nate. He retrieved the pain pills from his pocket and shook out two for Nate.

"I'm going to go home," Adam said.

The guys stopped talking and stared at him.

"Don't you think you need to take it easy?" Morgan asked.

"You're not in any condition to drive," Nate said. "Neither am I."

"I don't care. I'll hire a driver if I have to."

"What's so important that you need to go home this week?" Cade asked.

Adam swallowed, debated telling a lie. "I need to see—" He broke off, swallowed again and went with the truth. "I think either my father or brother had something to do with the accident. I spoke with the driver of the gray car before he croaked. Someone paid him to kill me."

"What?" Cade demanded.

J.T.'s brows rose. "Who?"

"You believe that nutcase?" Morgan asked in clear disbelief.

226

"You think your family would try to kill you?" J.T. asked.

The questions came quick and fast, and finally Adam held up his hand in protest. "I'm sorry. I can't go into details—"

"Dammit, Adam. We're your family," Morgan said. "You need to tell us what's going on."

"We're involved, whether you like it or not." Cade glowered at him. "Why would you want to visit your family if you think one of them is trying to kill you?"

"Tell them," Nate said in a gruff voice. "They're right. You're closer to them than anyone else. You guys have been together for a long time, gone through both good and bad. If you can't trust them, then there's no hope for the band continuing."

Adam considered Nate's suggestion. Secrecy about Kokopelli was a given. It was something private, something most people wouldn't believe and others assumed was a legend. He glanced at Nate, saw the encouragement on his face. A quick glimpse of his other friends showed curiosity and determination. Clearly, they wouldn't leave until he spilled the truth. Finally, he nodded and started to unbutton his shirt.

"Whoa!" J.T. held up his hand. "If this is turning kinky, I'm out of here."

Adam barked out a laugh, then groaned at the throb of

his head. "Shut up," he muttered. "Don't make me laugh. It hurts. I need to show you something." He peeled off the shirt so they could all see the tattoo that had grown and colored during the last month. "This is a Kokopelli tattoo. Actually, it's more than a tattoo. It's a mark or brand that tells others of my powers."

"What the hell are you talking about?" J.T. asked.

"I'm Kokopelli. You must have heard of the hunchback who travels through the Southwest making sure both the crops and women are fertile?"

"Bullshit," Morgan said.

"It's not," Nate said. "Have you noticed how the trees are flourishing on this street? How the flowers in the gardens here at the motel have flowered, almost overnight? That is not a tattoo. Take a close look. It's not inked onto the skin."

"A tattoo of that magnitude would take months to complete," Cade said slowly.

"And Adam has been with us or with Nate most of that time," J.T. finished.

"You're really Kokopelli?" Morgan's voice still held skepticism.

"Yeah. When I lived at home, I was Kokopelli. Then my father found out about me. They performed a ceremony, and I don't know how or why, but the mark faded from my chest overnight. It was the weirdest thing," Adam said. "They didn't like a gay Kokopelli. Everyone shunned me, and it was easier for me to leave than put up with the abuse."

"So why has the Kokopelli come back?" Morgan asked. "What does it mean?"

"I don't know. I need to talk to them, ask questions. If I see them in person, I can read their body language and get a better handle on what's happening."

Cade nodded. "I'm still not sure I buy into this Kokopelli stuff, but I agree that you need to check out things at home. We'll hire a car and I'll drive."

"I'll go and organize it," Morgan said, jumping to his feet.

"We'll leave tomorrow morning," J.T. added.

"What? You're all coming with me?" Adam asked, part of him in shock.

"Hell, yeah," Cade said. "You need someone to watch your back."

"Thanks." A touch on his hand claimed Adam's attention.

"I told you they were family," Nate said. "You can trust them."

Adam nodded, an ache in his chest and the tightness at the back of his eyes choking him up. He'd never expected this sort of support.

"You would do anything for them," Nate said quietly, watching the other band members as they discussed a plan of attack. "They know that and want to return the favor, show how much they care."

It was true. A lone tear trickled down his cheek, and he hurriedly swiped it away before anyone noticed. He coughed to clear the obstruction in his throat. "Ah, Cade?"

"Yeah?"

"If you're having sex with your lady, you should be extra careful from now on. Keep her well away from me."

"Why?" Cade asked, frowning at him with suspicion. "She didn't make a pass at you, did she?"

Nate laughed, and Adam shot him a wink. "No," Adam said. "I'm saying that unless you want to have a kid, you should be very careful. I'm telling you that Kokopelli's powers are real. They work."

Cade made a panicked, almost choking sound deep in his throat. "Well, fuck me," he said finally.

"Just as well you're serious about her," Nate said drowsily.

Morgan chuckled. "Thanks for offering, Cade. We might have to take advantage of your offer if we intend to keep Adam around."

"You...I didn't mean literally, asshole." Cade rolled his

eyes in horror.

A hoot of laugher escaped J.T., and it started them all off. They didn't stop laughing for a long time.

"J.T., ARE YOU SURE you want to keep driving?" Adam asked. "One of us can take over for you."

"Instead of worrying about me, you should work on a plan. What if your brother or your father really does have something to do with the dead assassin guy? If that's the case, we're driving into danger."

Nate leaned between the front seats of the SUV. "One thing I don't understand—if you used to be Kokopelli, how did a ceremony transfer the job to your brother?"

"There's an element of mystique about Kokopelli," Adam said, turning around to look at them. "Usually the powers go to the oldest male in our family. After my father reached the retirement age, for some reason the Kokopelli tattoo appeared on me. It caused problems in our family. My father accused my mother of straying, and my brother Justin hated me. The gossip spread through the village like mass hysteria. People started to whisper about my mother and my brother. The gossip killed her. She caught pneumonia and seemed to give up the fight to live.

"My brother had blood tests done, and there's no doubt he's my full brother."

"Yeah, but did the villagers believe it?" J.T. asked. "I know what small town gossip is like. It carries on for years, constantly resurrected and embroidered."

Adam snorted. "Justin looks like my father, but they still doubted, at least until I left. Anyway, getting back to the time when my father kicked me out of home. Once the news I was gay came out, they wanted me gone. In the records, they found a ceremony which was acceptable under radical circumstances. The villagers voted in favor of the ceremony, they performed it at midnight under the full moon and, as I said, the next day Justin bore the Kokopelli tattoo. I haven't had contact with my family or visited home since then."

"Fuck, that's archaic," Cade muttered. "My brother and I raised hell when we were kids. We were always in trouble, but my family would never force me to leave home."

"You're not gay," Adam pointed out, his voice holding a touch of bitterness, despite the fact he'd told himself he'd made peace with the past.

"We haven't kicked you out of the band," Morgan reminded him.

"You need me," Adam said.

"Hate to tell you this, hotshot, but everyone is

replaceable." Cade winked at Morgan and Nate. "We only put up with you because your pretty face brings in the chicks."

Adam flipped him the bird and leaned forward. "The turnoff is on the right."

J.T. indicated right and left the freeway. The scrubby plains and the red dirt looked so familiar. Adam swallowed, concentrating fiercely on even breathing. He focused on a pronghorn, watching the antelope lift its head and bound away when their vehicle approached. A tight knot of apprehension filled his gut, and the feelings rushed in on him. He remembered how he'd felt when his father had told him in a cold voice to leave. The finality in his father's words—the inherent disappointment. He thought he'd shed the pain, the sense of isolation and betrayal, and left it in the past. Not so. One glimpse of the familiar scenery, the smell of the sage, and it felt as if he were that kid again, the one who'd battled with sexual identity and heavy responsibilities as Kokopelli.

Wasn't it just a kick in the head, knowing that somehow the responsibility had returned to him? A full circle.

A hand squeezed his shoulder. "You okay?" Nate's soft voice whispered across his ear.

"Yeah." Adam sighed. "No. I thought I'd come to terms with it all, but coming home has brought everything back.

My father was cold. At the end, he acted as if I was a stranger."

"What about your brother?" J.T. asked. "It sounds as if he had a rough deal too."

"Justin and I didn't get on. We argued a lot as kids, with Justin lording it over me, saying he was special because he'd become Kokopelli after our father. When the tattoo formed on me instead, he didn't handle it well."

"Neither did the people around you," Nate said. "You have nothing to feel guilty about. You don't need to apologize to anyone or do anything just because of that tattoo on your chest. You're a musician, Adam, and a damn good one. You're living the life you want, and don't let any of them tell you different."

Adam swallowed at the heartfelt friendship and loyalty in Nate's words. Dare he say love? He swallowed again and wiped the palms of his hands on his jeans. Nerves jumped inside him, making him feel as if he'd pulled an all-nighter and subsisted on coffee throughout the night. "Take the next turn on the left."

"Who are we going to see first? Your father or your brother?"

"Justin, probably, although I have no idea where he lives. I doubt he still lives at home."

"Why don't we stop and ask these kids up ahead?" J.T.

asked. "I'll do the talking, in case they recognize you."

"I've been gone for almost six years. I don't think they'd know me."

J.T. slowed and pressed the control to lower his window. "Hey, can you guys tell me where Justin James lives?"

The teen's dark eyes widened as he glanced past J.T. and sighted Adam. "Mr. James lives on the other side of town. Second road on the right after you pass the gas station."

The kid behind him whispered something, and Adam's stomach bucked, his mind back in his teenage days when everyone gossiped about him and his family. Mostly about him.

"You guys are Stampede," the first teen blurted.

"Yes," J.T. replied.

"Are you doing a gig here?"

"Not this time," J.T. said easily. "We're visiting friends. Thanks for the directions." With a hand raised in farewell, he accelerated smoothly before the teens could fire more questions at them.

"I can't believe the kids out here have heard of us," Adam said, shock still rippling through him. They must know he was Justin's brother, and yet they hadn't mentioned a thing about his...history. Weird. The father he remembered would have banned anything and everything related to his music. The gay one. The fag. He

SHELLEY MUNRO

still remembered the jeers, the taunts.

"Stop panicking," Nate said. "Take some deep breaths."

"There's nothing wrong with me. I don't need handling."

"If there's nothing wrong, then why are you snapping?" Morgan asked.

"I'm not."

"Jeez, Adam. Don't go all childish on us," J.T. said. "It sucks the way your father treated you. Think of it this way. He did you a favor, because if he hadn't pushed you out, you wouldn't have met us."

"You're right," Adam said. "My head is telling me that, but—" He broke off, shaking his head. "Never mind. There's the turn."

A few minutes later, the road came to an end in front of a huge two-story house.

"Big brother did good," Cade said.

"The village looks better than I remember too." Adam climbed out of the SUV, holding on to the door to keep upright. This house must have cost a fortune. Where had the money come from? The duties of Kokopelli would keep him too busy to hold down the sort of job Justin would need to afford a property like this.

Nate limped around the SUV to join him. Despite the fact that they were out in the open where the others and the locals might see them, Nate hugged him roughly, then stepped back.

"Things have changed around here. Money…"

"Maybe he won the lottery." Nate shrugged as if he didn't think it was a big deal.

"Maybe." Quite frankly, Adam didn't care about money. All he needed was enough to survive. He didn't need material possessions to showcase his wealth to others. But the obvious prosperity here surprised him.

"Are we going to do this?" Cade asked.

"Maybe I should go in alone," Adam said.

Nate tensed. "Hell, no."

"I agree. We're going with you," J.T. said in an implacable tone.

Morgan gestured at him. "Let's go."

Cade strode ahead and pounded on the red door with his fist, ignoring the ornate knocker. "Move it along," he said. "Time's a wastin'."

Adam hovered beside Nate, making sure he didn't trip. Not that there was anything to stumble on. The footpath appeared in pristine condition, as did the pots of purple and white pansies.

The door opened, and a young woman stood in the doorway, a slender figure with long, dark hair. She wore black trousers and a body-hugging turquoise top.

"Look at the way she's cradling her stomach. She's pregnant," Nate murmured in his ear.

Adam had no idea who she was and had never seen her before. "Is Justin here?"

"I'll get him for you." She frowned at the other men, hesitated, then said, "Do you want to come in and wait?"

Footsteps sounded behind the woman. "Who is it, Lara?"

Adam stepped forward. "Justin." It was the first time he'd seen his brother since the night he'd left. He looked older, more polished, and wore a smart suit. Unfamiliar glasses perched on his brother's nose, and the shadows beneath his eyes indicated Justin hadn't slept well recently.

The color seeped from his face. "Adam?"

Adam cocked his head, watching his brother closely. "We need to talk." He noticed the way Justin glanced at his friends and frowned slightly.

"This is Nate, Cade, Morgan and J.T.," Adam said.

"Come in," Justin said, standing back. "This is my wife Lara."

"Lara." Adam entered the large tiled foyer, suddenly glad of the guys at his back. He caught the gaze Justin flicked at his jeans and T-shirt and barely restrained his snarl. It seemed some things hadn't changed. His brother was still a pretentious snob.

"Have you seen our father?"

"No, I decided to see you first." Adam didn't like to admit he was afraid of the reception he might receive from his father. He'd known Justin would at least want to lord it over him and sneer at his obvious lack of wealth. Adam didn't care about that. He needed information. "I need to talk to you about Kokopelli."

"Not in front of outsiders," Justin snapped.

Adam straightened. "They know."

A hiss escaped Justin, his dark eyes flashing with anger. "You don't tell outsiders."

His brows rose. "They're my best friends. My family."

"Give it a break," Cade cut in, looking as if he might roll his eyes. "Who's gonna believe this story anyway? A figure who goes around promoting fertility. Yeah, right." He sniggered.

"Don't mock what you don't understand," Lara said, her eyes flashing with a hint of temper.

"Quite right, my love." Justin wrapped his arm around his wife's waist, the softening of his face and faint smile telling Adam his brother truly loved this woman. This was a radical change for a man who used to go through women like tissues. It made him wonder what sort of woman his new sister-in-law was, because somehow he didn't think Justin would change.

"Shall I make tea or coffee?" Lara asked.

"Coffee would be great," Adam said.

Lara inclined her head and disappeared through a doorway on their left.

"We can talk in here." Justin pulled a white handkerchief from his pocket and wiped his brow. Now that his wife had gone, he seemed ill at ease. Nervous, even. He led them into a room overlooking a valley, the range of mountains beyond jutting up like sharp teeth on the horizon. A sluggish river meandered along the valley floor, and a small herd of elk picked its way across, stopping to graze now and then.

"Nice view," Adam said. "Have you lived here long?"

"About two years," Justin said.

Cade, Morgan, J.T. and Nate took possession of chairs and waited expectantly for Adam to get to the important stuff. When he hesitated, Cade coughed, jerking his head at Justin. Adam glared at him. It wasn't exactly something he could blurt out. He needed to work his way into the subject.

"Someone tried to kill Adam. Did you do it?" J.T. demanded.

So much for diplomacy. Adam started to stay something, but Nate's swift shake of head stopped him. He scrutinized Justin then and caught a strange expression on his face.

"You know something," Cade said in disbelief.

"You tried to kill your brother." Morgan looked as if he wanted to whack Justin into the wall.

"You put all of us in danger," Nate snapped.

"Why?" While Adam had considered the possibility, he hadn't really believed until he'd seen the guilt on his brother's face. "Why the fuck would you do that to me when I haven't stepped foot near here since the day I left?"

His brother refused to look at him, although, to Adam's surprise, he answered. "I was losing my powers. My tattoo has faded. It's barely visible now, but no one in the village has come forward to claim the office of Kokopelli." Justin wiped his hands down his thighs.

Clammy palms. He might wipe those, but he couldn't rid his forehead of the telltale tension without dragging out his handkerchief again.

Adam stared, incredulous. "Why didn't you just contact me? We could have talked."

"But I didn't know where to find you."

"Bullshit," Nate snapped. "You knew where to send people to shoot and attack Adam."

"I...I..." Justin trailed off, his face pale and panicked.

"Leave Justin alone." The feminine voice stopped Morgan and Cade's grumbling curses. "I've rung your father. He'll arrive soon, so they can't hurt you without witnesses."

Nate turned on her. "What, it's all right for him to attempt to kill Adam?" The sting of temper shaded his words.

Lara placed a tray of cups and a coffeepot on a low wooden table before turning around to glare at them. "Justin has made mistakes, and he's truly sorry. At least he tried to call off the assassin."

"Oh, yeah? And that makes it okay?" Cade sneered. "That damn assassin crashed into our van and tried to kill us."

Nate lurched to his feet, his fists clenched. "You're jealous of Adam."

Adam stared at his brother, unable to wrap his head around the truth. Justin hadn't denied a thing. How could Justin hate him? He hadn't been around to get in the way or interfere. He hadn't been part of the Kokopelli legend, hadn't cared about the legend or even thought about it until the tattoo had started to reform on his chest.

Morgan nailed Justin with a fierce glare and took a couple of steps toward him. "Don't hit him, Nate. I'd like that honor."

"No one is hitting anyone," Lara stated in a firm voice.

"You think it's all right for Justin to organize someone

to kill Adam? Adam left here when your father kicked him out. He has a new family now." Nate folded his arms over his chest. "Us."

Adam whipped off his T-shirt to display the Kokopelli. It glowed, the brilliant turquoise, red, blue and white vivid against his golden skin. He thumped his chest with his fist. "I didn't ask for this. We'll talk to Father. Maybe there's some way to transfer the Kokopelli again."

"No," Justin said. "I don't want the responsibility anymore."

"And yet you wanted it enough to need me dead."

A loud thump sounded at the entrance.

"That's probably your father," Lara said.

Justin shot a glance at Adam's chest before saying, "I'll get it."

"I'll get it," Cade said. "I don't trust you."

Justin hesitated, then shrugged. Cade arrived back a few moments later on the heels of an older man.

"Father," Justin said, a hint of panic in his voice.

"Justin." He turned to Adam, his eyes widening when he spied the Kokopelli on his chest. "Adam."

Adam inclined his head in a show of respect. "Father."

"You're back," his father said. "Good. That's good. It was time for you to return."

CHAPTER TWELVE

"HE'S NOT RETURNING," NATE snapped.

"No." A few years ago his father's words might have pleased Adam, but now he was older and realized acceptance came with an unspoken price. One he wasn't willing to pay. He owed the band and he wanted Nate in his life.

"You bear the badge of office."

"You find someone to take over, do the hocus-pocus or whatever you did last time to shift the tattoo to Justin. I'm not staying here." He strode to Nate's side and wrapped his arm around Nate's shoulders. "I have responsibilities to my friends and to Nate."

"You have a duty to your ancestors, to the villagers. You must not walk away and bring shame to our family."

Huh! He thought it was too late to worry about shame. As usual, his father wasn't listening. Time to make it clearer. He straightened and met his father's gaze directly, as an adult. "You can't make me stay."

"You would throw away hundreds of years of tradition because of a man?"

Adam's upper lip curled at the clear disgust in his father's tone. "You can say it, Father. He's my lover." Adam slipped on his T-shirt again.

"And what do you say about this?" his father asked Justin. "You no longer have powers, yet you didn't say anything, didn't report to the elders." He ran his fingers through his long, gray hair, and Adam noticed the faint tremor of his father's hand.

"I don't understand," his father said. "It's true, for a long time the magic was absent." His piercing brown gaze zeroed in on Justin. "We were going to replace you, but after your marriage to Lara, conditions improved. The crops were healthy, so we changed our minds. I don't understand any of this."

"Ignoring Nate won't make him go away," Adam mocked, noting the way his father continued to look straight through Nate. Familiar pain swelled in his chest. He turned to Justin, spearing him a hard look. "I'm leaving with my friends now. I don't intend to return. I don't want the Kokopelli responsibilities. They're all yours. If you're gonna come after me, tell me now."

"You can't leave." His father's brows drew together, anger flattening his mouth to a firm line.

"Justin?" Adam ignored his father for the moment, more intent on his brother's reply. He wanted Justin's verbal agreement to leave him alone, to live his life as he chose, without the need to keep looking over his shoulder. His gaze drifted from Justin back to his father. When had his father shrunk? He'd never seemed so small. Justin towered over him.

"What are you talking about? Justin, what's he talking about?"

"Justin is responsible for several attempts on Adam's life," Nate snarled. "I think we should turn him in to the police."

"I second that," Cade said. "We should go."

Morgan nodded and stood. "Come near us again and we'll report you to the cops."

"You can't prove anything," Justin said.

"Maybe not, but we can make things uncomfortable for you," J.T. said.

"Who are these people?" his father demanded.

"My family," Adam said, realizing it was the truth. The band and Nate were his family, and he would do anything for them. He glanced at Nate. "Let's go. I've learned everything I needed to know."

"You can't just walk out," his father said. "We can talk about this."

"You have responsibilities now," Justin said. "I can't carry out Kokopelli duties. It wouldn't be right."

"We really did intend to ask you to return," his father said, his tone conciliatory now.

"Thanks, but I'll pass," Adam said, moving toward the door. Nate and the others followed.

"Adam, wait," his father snapped.

Adam kept walking without looking back. He was glad he'd faced both his father and brother. He hadn't fully realized how much bitterness he'd carried inside, the resentment he'd held close to his chest. He didn't have to stay, and that felt liberating. He had close friends, a new family and a man he loved and wanted to spend the rest of his life with. Now all he needed to do was tell Nate and make the commitment.

They piled into the SUV, and Morgan backed up and turned the vehicle. "Why don't we splurge and stop at one of the places we saw during the drive down? I don't feel like driving for too much longer today."

"Suits me," Cade said.

"What about your woman?" J.T. asked. "Won't she

expect you home, or is she out on the road again?"

"I told her we might be out of town overnight. She won't worry. Besides, I can ring her."

"Adam, what about the Kokopelli shit?" Morgan asked. "Is that gonna be a problem for us?"

"I did some research," Nate said. "According to the info I found on the Internet, Kokopelli was often seen as a wandering minstrel and traveled from town to town, playing his flute and spreading the fertility around. I figure if we're on the road playing at different venues, we're doing the same thing. Most of the legends I found on the net seemed to come from the Southwest, but that doesn't mean Kokopelli didn't travel farther afield."

"I like it." Cade grinned. "Bringing the legend into the future."

"We can be like that Pied Piper dude," J.T. said. "The chicks will follow us everywhere, except we'll be loving them instead of killing them off."

Morgan scratched his chin, his stubble rasping with the drag of his fingertips. "I don't think the chicks would like the comparison to rats."

"And the ones who are careless with birth control wouldn't like it so much," Adam added with a wry laugh.

"So that means if we keep you around, we need to suit up without fail," Cade said, a frown hinting at his seriousness.

"Yeah. I'm not kidding about it, either. Unless you're serious about the woman, make sure you take precautions."

"Does that mean I should never have sex again?" Nate asked.

"Man, don't say stuff like that," J.T. muttered before Adam could reply. "I love both of you, but I don't wanna know about your sex life."

Adam stared out the window at the scenery, the familiar hills and scrubby flats with the red rocks everywhere bringing a rush of memories. Confusion had filled him during his teenage years—lots of angst because of his sexual yearnings, and the pressure from his father and village elders when the Kokopelli had manifested on his chest. The weird thing was that he didn't remember the Kokopelli ever looking so colorful and vibrant. The one he'd had as a teenager had scarcely had any color, certainly none of the brilliant colors of this one. And the heat. He didn't recall the same amount of heat emanating from the Kokopelli. Sometimes it almost pulsed. He noticed the weird sensation when he stood close to Nate, and it had happened again when Lara had stood near him. He had no idea what it meant, but wasn't about to ask his father or Justin for advice.

"What happens if your brother comes after you again?"

Morgan asked.

"I don't think he will," Nate said before Adam could answer. "I watched him closely when we were there. I think he's genuinely sorry for his actions. Besides, I think he truly loves his wife. He couldn't take his eyes off her. I don't think he wants to do anything to jeopardize his relationship."

"When did you become so Mr. New Age Sensitive?" Cade demanded.

"Just because you go around with your head up your ass," Morgan said. "Some of us know how to pay attention."

Adam smirked while good-natured insults flew. Walking away was the right thing to do. With his friends around him, and his music, he'd manage to keep sane and maybe even do some good with Kokopelli along for the ride.

⁕⁕⁕

The Inn was a quiet lodge, a classy place where people came to take nature walks and fish in the nearby lake. The band sat out on the terrace with drinks in hand, watching the sun set and the sky color to a bright pink.

Footsteps heralded a new arrival, and Adam turned his head, stiffening when he saw who it was. "What do you want? Where's Justin?"

"How did you know where we were?" J.T. demanded.

Lara stared at him, her chin lifting in defiance. Long, dark hair flowed over her shoulders, and she glowed with good health. "I came alone. It wasn't difficult to find you. I know some of the people who work here. Besides, a couple of the local kids saw you come into the lodge."

Cade made a scoffing sound. "Did Justin send you to shoot Adam?"

"Justin is sorry for his actions. He told you that he tried to stop the contract, but couldn't. It's the truth."

"Yeah?" Adam shook his head in disbelief. "It's normal for one brother to shoot another."

"He wasn't thinking right. That's not what I came to say. You must return home. The people need you."

"I don't think so," Adam said. "My father told me to leave, and I did. I wasn't welcome then, and I sure as hell don't want to go back now."

"You must return."

"Didn't you hear him, darlin'?" Cade's brow furrowed. "He doesn't want to return. Hell, I don't blame him. It's not as if he could trust any of you not to shoot him in the back."

"You will return. Now," Lara barked and she pulled a handgun from her shoulder bag. The safety clicked as she thumbed it off.

"Whoa!" Morgan stood and backed up, putting himself in front of Adam. "Take it easy. Put the gun down."

Nate also stood, moving in his direction despite his injured leg, ready to shield him. All of his friends were ready to protect him. The knowledge made him realize how lucky he was to have their support.

He stood and faced Lara. "Go ahead and shoot me. I'm not going back."

"But you have to go back," Lara said with a trace of panic. "If you don't go back, Justin will have to take responsibility. I don't want that." The hand holding the gun trembled. "Is it so much to want a normal life for our baby?"

"Shooting me won't improve your lot." Adam pushed past Nate and Morgan and reached for the gun. "Give me the gun, Lara."

"Lara!" Justin rushed onto the terrace, his face red from exertion. "What are you doing? Put down the gun."

"He refused to return home. He needs to go home and take up the Kokopelli duties." Her hand shook, the gun wavering.

"Why?" Justin asked his wife. "Why is it so important to you?"

"I want a normal life again. One with you and me and

the baby. A life where you have a job you love. We can't have that if he doesn't return home."

"But you were so angry when I..." Justin glanced at him and away again. "When I did what I did. I don't understand why you've changed."

"Back then I thought you were Kokopelli. I love you. I didn't like you being Kokopelli, but I made the best of it. Now we have a chance for an ordinary life." The gun wobbled again. "If your brother doesn't return, your father will try every avenue to transfer Kokopelli back to you. All I want is a normal life and for our children to grow up without the pressure of knowing their father is Kokopelli. I don't want hate between my children. I don't want one to feel jealous of another because their grandfather is telling them stories of the importance of Kokopelli."

Tears ran down her face, and Adam suddenly felt sorry for her. She loved Justin and was willing to kill for a chance at a regular life. He understood the need to feel average. He'd tired of the pressure his father put him under, and the minute he hadn't met parental expectations, he'd been down the road. Yeah, he could understand Lara's panic. Surely there had to be a way to keep everyone happy? Justin, Lara, his father and the rest of the elders.

"Put the gun down, sweetheart. Shooting him isn't

going to make things better. Give me the gun." Justin edged closer.

Adam watched Lara's face, saw her distress. Kokopelli had shadowed his life from the day he was born. His gaze strayed to Lara's belly and her protective hand that crept down to caress it. Yeah, he understood.

"What if we worked together to tag team our father? We were talking about it on the way here. There's no reason why things have to be done the same way our father and grandfather did them."

Lara's hand trembled, and the gun lowered. "Together?"

"No," Nate snapped. "You can't trust them. They keep pointing guns at you."

Warmth suffused Adam, and he squeezed Nate's shoulder in silent reassurance. "I'm sure we can come to a solution to suit us all. It's not as if there's a rule book. Everything we know—"

Justin broke in, hope creeping into his face. "Has been passed on to us by Father. Do you think... Could we work together after everything that has happened?"

Adam leaned into Nate, breathing in his scent and feeling content. "Justin, do you still want me dead?"

"Hell, no!" Justin said without hesitation.

"What about you?" Nate demanded, glaring at Lara and the gun she still held at her side. "Do you want Adam dead?"

"Yeah," Cade said. "Why should we believe that either of you won't hurt Adam or one of us? You don't have a good track record."

"It's the stress, the expectation of the villagers," Lara said, finally clicking on the safety and placing the gun out of sight in her bag. "Last year, we went through a period where nothing went right. Crops failed. Several of the women who were pregnant lost their babies. Others had young children who died, and everyone started looking at Justin, whispering behind his back."

"I haven't always used the powers of Kokopelli in a responsible manner," Justin admitted. "Before I married Lara, I used to sleep with any woman who would accept me and I took money from everyone who wanted a piece of the legend. After I met Lara, things started to change. Lara transformed me, made me into a better person, and I realized the hate I'd directed toward you, the jealousy, was misplaced. I'm ashamed to say I tried to shoot you myself and then I paid an assassin to try to do the job for me. Then...I had second thoughts, but the man I'd paid to do the job wouldn't let me cancel."

J.T. snorted. "He's dead now. Consider the job canceled."

"How do I know you won't change your mind?" Adam

spoke the words that concerned them all.

Justin's face was sober. "I guess you don't, but I could give you a signed confession, if you like. If something happens, you'd have my written confession of guilt."

Adam glanced at Nate, then the others, and nodded. "That would work. Go home and write your confession. We'll meet here again tomorrow for lunch."

"We can come earlier," Lara said.

"No. Midday tomorrow, and we'll discuss how to stand against our father. Agreed?"

Justin extended his hand for Adam to shake. "It's a deal, but are you sure Father and the other elders can't transfer the Kokopelli again?"

"I don't think so," Adam said. "Because otherwise he would have done it earlier. He didn't approve of the way you did things, right?"

"He doesn't approve of our marriage," Lara said, "because after we married, Justin wouldn't listen to him anymore, wouldn't take his advice. Your father has been ill recently, which meant he backed off a little. He asked me to Google you on our computer at the house."

Good. They could do this. Both he and Justin could have fairly normal lives, doing exactly what they wanted. With him, Kokopelli would be on the road. Yeah, he'd take the powers to the people and reach farther than

Kokopelli had in any other generation. All they needed to do was cooperate as brothers, for once. "Tomorrow," Adam confirmed.

With a nod, Justin wrapped his arm around Lara's waist and guided her from the lodge.

"Anyone feel like a beer?" Morgan asked.

"Hell, yeah," Cade said. "Sounds like a plan." His cell rang and, after checking the screen, he answered it with a broad smile on his face. "Hi, sweetheart."

"Not for me," Adam said. "Nate and I are heading to our room."

"We are?"

"Yeah, we are. Don't expect to see us until the morning."

"Are you gonna have sex?" J.T. asked, waggling his eyebrows.

"That depends on Nate."

"Pregnant!" Cade blurted, halting all conversation. As they stared at him, his shock transformed, a brilliant grin lighting his blue eyes. "That's great, sweetheart. I'll be home in a couple of days." He paused, his grin widening, if anything. "No, I think it's wonderful. I'm happy about the baby. Okay. See you tomorrow." He hung up, his happiness clear for them all to see. "I'm gonna be a daddy. Who wants another drink?"

"I told you to be careful," Adam said.

257

"What's Susan gonna say?" Morgan taunted.

J.T. smirked. "You're gonna get in trouble."

"You happy about it?" Nate asked. At Cade's nod, Nate grinned, yanking him into a hug. "Congratulations, man. That's awesome."

"Hey, stop groping my man." Adam tugged Nate away and moved in to hug Cade. "Congratulations."

Cade beamed. "Who wants a drink?"

"We'll see you in the morning," Nate said without taking his gaze off Adam. The heat in his eyes melted Adam's lingering anxiety about how his lover felt about the day's events.

Everything would work out, and if it didn't, he had Nate and his friends to help him. They hustled to their room as quickly as Nate's leg and crutches would allow them. Adam closed the door and locked it with a sharp click.

"How's the leg?"

"A bit sore," Nate said.

"You need to relax. Take some more of the painkillers they gave you at the hospital."

"The painkillers make me sleepy."

"So?"

"I don't want to sleep." Nate sank onto the edge of the queen-size bed with a soft groan. "Not yet." He tugged off his boots and socks, stood briefly to slide out of his jeans and T-shirt and dropped on the bed again. "Why don't you come down here and join me?"

Adam felt a grin stretch his lips and didn't even try to hide the lust that roared through him. He was on the bed before he even realized he'd moved, grabbing Nate and wrapping his arms around his shoulders. Briefly, he wished he'd ripped off his clothes so he could enjoy the sensation of skin against skin, then their lips aligned. Adam lost his train of thought. He loved kissing Nate, loved his scent with the faint hint of soap and the contrast of beard and soft lips. They kissed for a long time, starting slowly and gradually deepening the contact, exploring with tongues and lips. If anyone had told him he'd have been satisfied with a mere kiss, he'd have told them they were talking out their ass. But with Nate, it was true. Just knowing Nate wanted to be with him, that he sought contact with him freely, brought satisfaction and made Adam feel warm inside.

"I love you, Nate." The words burst from him, taking him by surprise.

Nate blinked, and a smile spread from his eyes down to his mouth. "Yeah?"

"Is that all you have to say?" Nate could have returned the sentiment, at least. Adam thought Nate had feelings for him, but hearing the words would make things official.

Make it real.

"Why don't you get naked?"

Disappointment speared him. He wanted the words, plain and unembroidered. Patience, he told himself. Nate would get there soon, if not today, then another day. Adam pushed away from Nate and yanked his T-shirt over his head.

"Do it slow for me." Nate pushed up on his elbows and plumped a pillow to get comfortable. "I like seeing you get naked."

Adam glanced at Nate's erection and grinned. "Don't tell me you want music as well?"

"Another time."

"You could tell me what you're going to do to me. That would help me get in the mood."

Nate glanced at the defined bulge in his jeans and snorted. "You just want me to talk dirty."

"Yup." Adam scrambled out of his jeans or tried to. Moron! He'd forgotten to take off his boots. Cursing, he yanked up his jeans and stooped to remove his boots and socks. Seconds later, his jeans hit the ground, followed by his underwear. He paused, the breeze from the air conditioner flowing over his skin.

"I like seeing you naked too," Nate said. "I like knowing you have a hard-on for me. I like seeing your muscles and your tight ass. Your cock. The way your face flushes and your eyes glitter when you're with me." He scrutinized him closely, and Adam could literally feel the heat as Nate's gaze roved over his body. "Once I've studied you from the front, I'm gonna ask you to turn around so I get the full view."

"And then you're gonna get with the program and we're gonna fuck, right?" Adam heard the husky tone of his voice. He only ever spoke that way when he was alone with Nate and wanting. Needy.

"No. Next up I'm going to explore your body. Turn around for me. Yeah, just like that."

Adam could still feel Nate's gaze on his body and his ass when he turned to present his back. His skin prickled, and he sucked in his breath, then let it ease out.

"Nice," Nate said. "Let's see the front again."

Adam's breath caught when he saw the passion in Nate's face. Oh, yeah. Nate might not have said the words, but he felt the emotions. Maybe that was enough.

"Stop thinking so hard." Nate stood and closed the distance between them. He ran his tongue over the column of his neck, ending up near his ear. Adam shivered, his heart beating faster. Damn that felt good. Nate nuzzled the sensitive skin behind his ear with his lips, licked the same path and nibbled on his earlobe. Adam swallowed, his nerve endings singing with pleasure. Nate started murmuring to him, the whisper of warm air zinging arrows of heat to his cock.

"Nate," he whispered, hungry for more. His hands urged Nate closer.

"Adam, kiss me."

Any time. Adam turned his head, their lips colliding. This time, Nate plundered his mouth, his aggression signaling things were about to get serious. Fine with him. Adam grasped Nate's shoulders and hung on. Nate pushed him, and they fell to the bed in a tangle of limbs. Nate pulled away and grinned at Adam, trapping him against the mattress while he took tiny nips at Adam's neck. They were hard enough to send jolts through him, but Adam didn't think they'd mark his skin. Not that he cared if they did. The others knew they were a couple. No more sneaking around.

Nate worked down his body, starting out slow and careful with each new location and gradually building up the pressure until Adam squirmed and moaned his satisfaction. Under Nate's ministrations, his nipples pulled to tight, sensitive nubs. His Kokopelli burned. Adam's breathing became heavy, his nostrils flaring. Nate's scent wound through his senses, along with intense yearning.

"Nate, God…please suck my cock." Adam didn't care if he sounded desperate. Hell, he was desperate. Nate was driving him crazy, yet at the same time he'd never felt so wanted. So loved. His breath eased out with a hiss, then he dragged in a sharp inhalation when Nate moved down the bed. He wanted to cry when Nate bypassed his dick. Instead, his lover exerted pressure on his legs, silently requesting he part them.

His lips settled on Adam's inner thighs, and he nibbled and licked. A lover had never done that before. Who knew it would feel so damn good?

"Where are the condoms? Lube?" Nate asked.

Adam blinked, not registering the question at first because he was lost in a sensual haze.

"Adam?"

"Uh…side pocket of my bag." It was a struggle to string together the words. He watched the play of muscles as Nate ambled across the room to crouch by his overnight bag. He wasn't limping too badly. A suspicion grew. "Is your leg okay?"

"I'm not pain-free, if that's what you mean, but we're alive. Both of us. All of us. The doctor said I'd have a scar. I won't limp or anything. A scar is a small price to pay."

"Yeah, it is."

Nate approached the bed, tossing the lube and condoms

within easy reach. "Everything will work out." He sank onto the bed, his hand reaching for Adam's leg as if he needed to touch him. A compulsion. Love welled inside Adam. Oh, yeah.

"I love you so much. I'm so glad I chased you."

"I'm glad, too, although I was pissed with you at the time. You're real talkative tonight."

Adam smirked and glanced at Nate's dick. "Maybe you should give me something to do with my mouth."

"You think?"

"Yeah, that's what I think." Adam pushed Nate until he lay back on the bed. He stroked a finger down Nate's shaft before he licked across the swollen glans at the top. Seeking Nate's gaze and maintaining it, he opened his mouth and surrounded the tip. His tongue collected the hint of pre-come before he started gentle suction.

"Feels good." Nate's fingers curled into his scalp, pressing and releasing until Adam wanted to purr. He hummed around Nate's cock, wanting to give the pleasure back tenfold.

"Enough," Nate said. "I want to come inside you." He pulled away, breathing hard, arousal glittering in his eyes. He reached for the lube. "Time to get serious."

"'Bout time."

Nate grinned at his lover. Adam loved him. He still

couldn't understand how he'd been so lucky to have two great loves. For the last few weeks, he'd felt comfortable in the knowledge he was with Adam. He loved him and was happy. He'd come to the realization it was okay to love someone other than Rosa. His heart was big enough to love both Rosa and Adam, and he knew she would want his happiness. Nate squirted lube onto his fingers and set the bottle aside. "You ready?"

"Hell, yeah."

"Face-to-face." Nate wanted to see Adam's expression when he admitted his love. He wanted to see the shine of happiness, needed Adam to see the love on his face. Unable to resist, Nate guided Adam's cock to his mouth and took him inside. The salty taste of pre-come filled his mouth, made him decide to hurry when he'd originally intended to take things slow and make Adam crazy with need.

He skimmed his finger over Adam's entrance, watching his face the entire time.

"You make me feel hot," Adam whispered. "I want you so much." He shivered when Nate dipped a finger inside him. Nate continued to tease and stroke and leaned over Adam, seeking his mouth.

They kissed, lips sipping and tasting, the sparks flaring between them into passion, need making Nate hurry his schedule along. Adam's warm channel clenched around his finger, and Nate added another, stretching Adam for his possession.

"Don't need much stretching," Adam said. "I need you."

"Are you sure?" Nate thought they might be talking about something other than sex. Didn't matter—he had that angle covered too. As far as Nate was concerned, they were a couple. Removing his fingers, he grabbed a condom and rolled it on. He lined up and pushed, taking it easy and watching Adam's face for the slightest discomfort.

"Don't hold back."

Taking Adam at his word, he thrust until he was fully impaled. "Adam," he murmured, savoring the squeeze of Adam's warm channel around his cock. "*Adam*." He wanted to make sure he had his lover's full attention.

"Do we have to talk now?"

Nate's lips twitched. "Yeah, we do."

Adam squirmed a little, his hands reaching down to fist his erection. "What?"

"I love you." Nate pulled back and thrust. "I." He retreated, then pushed forcibly enough to make Adam grunt. "Love. You."

"Good," Adam said, his eyes glowing with delight.

Nate increased his pace, submerging himself in the pleasure, the tight grip of Adam's body. He used Adam hard, and Adam encouraged it, grunting and groaning, demanding. He held back long enough to angle his strokes. Adam shuddered, pulling hard at his cock. He shuddered again and groaned, semen splattering his chest. With Adam still flexing around his cock, Nate let go, his orgasm rushing through him. Long seconds later, he collapsed against Adam's sweaty body.

"I love you, Adam."

"About time." Adam's grin faded. "We can do this, be together."

"There's nowhere else I'd rather be," Nate said, and he meant it with all of his heart. The future with Adam and his Kokopelli magic didn't scare him. In fact, he looked forward to the challenge. He'd found love again and he couldn't be happier.

THANK YOU FOR READING *Seeking Kokopelli*. Please turn the page to read excerpts from Lone Wolf and Fallen Idol.

Shelley

Excerpt – Lone Wolf

This book contains a young werewolf intent on seduction, an older werewolf determined to resist said seduction, werewolf politics and brutality, a little spilled blood, and hot, naked manlove in the great outdoors.

One glimpse of the stern man wearing the Yellowstone polo shirt and faded jeans and Corey's heart, the traitorous organ, jerked into a pitter-patter jig of excitement. Oh, he'd imagined himself in lust before but never like this—a punch to the gut and breath-stealing desire tracking straight to his cock. Despite his stern face and the quickly veiled shock, the guy rated extra hot on the hawt scale.

Tall and muscular. His short dark hair showed off the

strong planes of his face. Intense gray eyes flashed a sexy glare each time they focused on him. His mouth...well, a set of full lips like his weren't for mere kissing. They'd stretch perfectly around a cock. Without warning, Corey craved a sight of R.J. on his knees, mouth wrapped around *his* dick.

Yeah, in the near future he'd make his fantasies real.

Somehow.

After all, a challenge provided a fun way of spicing up life.

He glanced away, intuition telling him the sexy man stared after him. The temptation to twitch his butt pulled at him. He resisted, not wanting to overplay his hand. The anticipation of the chase was part of the fun. There'd be plenty of time for seduction since his parents' wishes put him in this no-town dump for the next three months.

A scowl burst to life at the reminder. Who the hell wanted to run around in a fur coat anyway? The memory of the pain and sheer savagery of shifting to wolf form brought a shudder of horror. Shoving the past away, he boarded the yellow bus and took possession of an empty seat. He'd noticed the others on the plane.

They'd taken one peek at him and judged by appearance, deeming his Goth makeup and apparel weird. A couple of the girls had treated him as if he carried cooties. A huff

269

of contempt layered with humor escaped. Little did they know they were safe from his lecherous ways.

The males—now that was another matter entirely.

Park Ranger Cutie stowed the last of the bags in the compartment at the rear of the bus. From where he sat, Corey watched him surreptitiously, appreciating the smooth flex and bulge of biceps each time he hefted a bag from the luggage trolley. Giggling from two of the girls told Corey he wasn't the sole audience of this show. The girls were out of luck, however, because judging by the flicker of awareness he'd witnessed earlier, he stood a better chance of scoring. If he wasn't mistaken, Park Ranger Cutie preferred men, which suited Corey fine.

An older man boarded the bus, clipboard in hand. Park Ranger Cutie took possession of the driver's seat. "Welcome to Yellowstone. I'm Hal Price-Jones, the director of the summer program. R.J. Blake here is our driver. He's my second-in-command and the person you'll come into contact with most on a day-to-day basis. We'll have a meeting tonight after dinner where R.J. and I will go through the rules and schedule. Our program will start officially tomorrow."

R.J. Blake lifted a hand in acknowledgment and turned away to start the bus. Corey pulled his sunglasses from his shirt pocket, placed them on and sprawled back in his seat. Most people would assume him asleep and leave him alone.

His thoughts drifted. Nine months ago his parents had informed him he'd spend his summer in Yellowstone. They expected him to ignore his art and learn to turn furry, enabling them to concentrate on consolidation with a neighboring pack. He'd tried objecting, promising to keep a low profile. His father said he was a smart-ass and he didn't trust him to behave in a manner befitting a pack leader's son. The consolidation was important and nothing could derail the talks. Nothing.

When calm reasoning failed, Corey had rebelled worse than usual. During full moon, when the call to shift pulled stronger than normal, his rage at his father's edicts fucked with his control. The infallible suppression drugs failed to hold him to human form and he'd partially shifted.

Corey fidgeted on the hard seat. Sweat beaded on his brow as his mind skittered through the terror again. The scrunching sounds. The musky scent of wolf. The agony when his bones and muscles warred with his mind. His gut roiled, the memories pounding him like a giant metal mallet. No wonder he lacked enthusiasm for this Yellowstone experience. Each nightmare replayed the shitload of pain.

Bad enough hiding in the gay closet, but having

a resident wolf writhing inside him sucked great big donkey's balls.

Someone tapped him on the back. Corey ignored the interruption until the person grasped his shoulder and yanked insistently.

"What do you want?" Corey demanded.

"Aren't you looking forward to the next three months?" a breathless feminine voice asked.

Great. Just great. "I didn't want to come. My father decided to send me here in punishment." Corey opened his eyes, part of him curious. His appearance normally put off people.

"Ooh, what did you do?" The breathless voice belonged to a vivacious blonde. Her clothes screamed popular cheerleader. Perkiness seeped out of her pores in puke-inducing waves.

"Did you break a pack law? Why is your father punishing you? All my friends applied to attend. They were pissed when they missed out." Her redhead friend sat beside her like a matching bookend, apart from the hair color.

Corey inspected his fingernails for chipped polish before deigning to reply. Not too bad. The nail polish cost heaps but possessed great staying power. "According to my father, I'm an embarrassment."

The two cheerleaders leaned forward, their blue eyes rounding in fascination. "Why? What did you do?"

"I like art. My father thinks it's sissy." Luckily none of the pack was aware of his preference for the male sex. The discovery would likely get him kicked out of the pack. The two teens craned forward even farther.

Most guys would have taken the opportunity to peer down their blouses. Corey wasn't that guy. "Also, I don't play nice." He peeled back his lips to display sharp teeth. "I eat little girls like you for dinner."

They giggled.

"That's what we thought," the blonde whispered, glancing over her shoulder to learn if any of the others were eavesdropping.

Corey rolled his eyes. The drugs didn't kill their senses, merely muted them and stole their ability to shift.

They were frickin' werewolves. Of course they were listening.

"We're best friends." She lowered her voice. "We do everything together. *Everything*." She blew him a kiss while her redhead friend winked at him.

Christ in a camper van. They wanted a threesome. With him. His wolf stirred. Oh hell. Not now! He sucked in a breath through his mouth and concentrated on his current painting, recreating each brushstroke in his mind.

"Are you okay?" one of the girls asked.

"Yeah. I...ah...get motion sickness sometimes."

"I'll open the window," one of the girls said. "The fresh air always helps me."

"Thanks." Finally his wolf subsided, and wrung out, Corey slumped lower on the seat.

"Better?"

"Yeah. Thanks." What the hell would happen once he stopped taking the drugs? The possible answers scared him.

The unknown.

His father really would disown him if he caused the pack embarrassment, and his problems would increase because the drugs didn't stop wolves craving the company of like. No matter how much he fought the desire, eventually his inner wolf drove him crazy and he had to return to visit his parents and the rest of the pack. A sort of a recharge because his wolf only rested easy when he had frequent contact with other werewolves.

"So what do you think?" Both girls beamed at him, fluttering their eyelashes in well rehearsed flirtation.

"I'll keep your offer in mind." Heck no. Never. Corey wouldn't touch them even if they paraded naked in front of him. The warning on the director's face when he glowered over his shoulder at them proved unnecessary.

"I'm tired. I'm going to sleep." He turned away and pretended to nap. Art. He needed to concentrate on his artwork because if he didn't, his wolf would push him again, despite the suppression pills.

Gah! How the heck was he gonna survive the next three months?

Visit Yellowstone National Park in Lone Wolf
www.shelleymunro.com/books/lone-wolf/

EXCERPT – FALLEN IDOL

THIS SCI-FI, FUTURISTIC ROMANCE contains a friends-to-lovers story plus reality shows of the future and several humorous sidekicks. It is a story of hope and despair and happy endings...

After climbing the dark stairwell, he exited on the fourth floor. There were six apartments on each floor. Rafi stalked down the wide passage toward number four, anticipation and apprehension skipping around inside him. Hell, seeing Roberto again was going to put him back at square one, ripping the scars from his wounded heart. But the idea of not seeing him—that was even worse.

He turned the corner and came to a halt. A pyramid of

empty vroom flasks littered the passage outside number four. Rafi frowned and strode to the door. Vroom was a rough liquor produced on the planet Marchant. People became addicted to it if they weren't careful. Eyesight was affected. In extreme cases blindness occurred along with lack of coordination and muscle wastage. The muscle melted away, replaced by excess fat. Rafi checked the pile of bottles again and shook his head. Surely this pile didn't belong to Roberto. He knocked on the door.

"What the hell do you want?" a masculine voice demanded. "Go away."

Rafi pounded a little harder, a tiny grin playing across his lips. Roberto's voice. Familiar, it brought back memories. The husky growl still made his cock jump with anticipation. Rafi's grin died. *Friend's box, remember?* Roberto wasn't interested in him in that way and all the wishing in the world wouldn't change the facts.

"Go the fuck away!" Roberto's rough voice rumbled through the door, slightly slurred but definitely recognizable.

Rafi shuddered at the abrasive texture of his friend's sexy reply. He'd never met a male who turned him on so quickly with just a word. After taking a deep breath, Rafi knocked again.

The door flew open.

"I told you before, man. I have nothing left. You've taken everything."

Rafi gaped at his friend. He was still tall and dark, but the bronzed god from his memory had vanished. Roberto was pale as a ghost. An overweight ghost. His muscles had disappeared, sinking into inches of blubbery fat. The sight of Roberto's bare chest and protruding gut made Rafi faintly nauseous so he glanced at his friend's face instead. His dark hair was long, scruffy and lank as though it hadn't been washed for weeks. And his face—hell his beautiful face was bloated and puffy. One bloodshot blue eye scowled at him while the other was black and almost swollen shut. Roberto's jaw was swollen too, and when Rafi studied his body again, he noticed bruises. Someone had bashed his friend and done a pretty good job of it.

"Roberto," Rafi said. He stood in the open doorway, uncertain for once in his life. He still didn't know where to look. Didn't Roberto have some clothes? That belly...it... Hell! It needed camouflage. Really badly. Rafi stared with fascinated horror as Roberto's belly jiggled when he inhaled.

His crew would have gaped with open mouths if they'd seen their captain appearing so indecisive. In the past, the two men would have exchanged a quick hug and clapped each other over the back. Rafi would have savored the moment as he usually did. He'd imagined the feel of Roberto's arms around him from the moment he'd decided to look his friend up between trips to the outer territories. Instead, there was awkwardness. Rafi didn't know what the hell to do. It was difficult looking at that blubber, but touching it? He shuddered inwardly and continued to hover outside the apartment. Part of him wanted to leave, to run away, but no, he couldn't do that. He refused to run away. His legs remained firmly planted outside the apartment while his mind told him to deal with it. No matter what, or how he looked, Roberto was still his friend.

"Rafi?"

Rafi tensed and steeled himself, forcing his real feelings deep so nothing showed from the outside. "Yeah, man. I stopped by the Gratham Apartments. One of the security men said you'd moved here." Not bad. His voice had sounded calm. Even.

"I don't suppose you'd leave if I asked you?" A tinge of shame colored Roberto's cheeks and his gaze slid away to stare at the floor.

Rafi forced himself to look his friend in the face. He was so...so... Hell, he reminded Rafi of a bloated whale. His gaze flitted across Roberto's face before darting over his friend's shoulder to study what he could of the apartment.

Another heap of opaque vroom flasks lay beside a wooden chair. The apartment was filthy and offended Rafi's nose. Soy dog wrappers littered the cheap plastic table. An open suitcase lay on the floor and the contents were strewn across the grubby gray floor in haphazard heaps. Rafi gave a cautious sniff before frowning. The smell could be coming from Roberto. He wasn't certain, but whatever the source, it was disgusting.

Rafi straightened and forced himself to look Roberto in the face again. "Why would I leave? Roberto, I came to see you." Roberto was his friend, and he was a friend in need.

Roberto didn't look convinced. "My name's Bob," he said. "I was born Bob and looks like I'll die Bob." Bitterness shaded his voice. "Call me Bob, like you used to when we were kids."

"Ah, sure." Rafi frowned. What the hell was going on? What had happened to his friend since his well-publicized injury? Roberto had always acted with confidence and known what he wanted from life. Ambitious from childhood, he'd set his mind on becoming a successful sex competitor and focused on his goal one hundred percent until he'd succeeded. He hadn't minded when Bob had wanted everyone to call him by his stage name. Rafi knew about being consumed by a dream, wanting to live it and become immersed in the success, which is why he'd understood Roberto. Rafi had always wanted to explore the uncharted territories. Maybe one day.

Since it didn't look as though Bob was going to let him inside, Rafi took matters into his own hands. He stalked past Roberto...Bob and recoiled at the stench. Gasping, he headed straight for the window.

"Won't open. It's nailed shut," Bob said seconds before Rafi attempted to open it.

Rafi turned to glance at his friend again. "Man, you need to do a little cleaning." His eyes streamed and he breathed shallowly through his mouth, trying to filter out the worst of the smell. Didn't work. "And you need a bath."

"Keeps the debt collectors away." Bob's top lip curled upward and he shrugged with unconcern. "Most of them." His blasé attitude was spoiled when he winced. Obviously the bruises on his body were still painful.

"Get cleaned up and I'll buy you a meal." Rafi was starting to feel pissed with his friend. He'd been looking forward to seeing Roberto, and even though he'd known Roberto wasn't interested in him in the same way, he'd expected to slip right into their easy friendship. Rafi's gaze slid across Roberto's pale, bloated face. This man was a stranger.

"Go out?" Bob made a theatrical gesture with his hands and struck a pose, one Rafi had seen him make onstage. He remembered the surge of jealousy he'd felt when Roberto's female partner had trailed her hands over Roberto...ah...Bob's tanned, muscular body when he'd stood in exactly the same way. Yeah, they'd looked great together on the stage but it hadn't lessened Rafi's longing. He'd imagined thrusting into Bob, running his hands over the smooth muscles, clutching the weight of his cock in his hands...

"I don't have a thing to wear," his friend said in a harsh voice.

Travel to the future with Rafi and Bob
www.shelleymunro.com/books/fallen-idol

ABOUT AUTHOR

USA Today bestselling author Shelley Munro lives in Auckland, the City of Sails, with her husband and a cheeky Jack Russell/mystery breed dog.

Typical New Zealanders, Shelley and her husband left home for their big OE soon after they married (translation of New Zealand speak - big overseas experience). A twelve-month-long adventure lengthened to six years of roaming the world. Enduring memories include being almost sat on by a mountain gorilla in Rwanda, lazing on white sandy beaches in India, whale watching in Alaska, searching for leprechauns in Ireland, and dealing with ghosts in an English pub.

While travel is still a big attraction, these days Shelley is most likely found in front of her computer following another love - that of writing stories of contemporary and paranormal romance and adventure. Other interests include watching rugby (strictly for research purposes), cycling, playing croquet and the ukelele, and curling up with an enjoyable book.

Visit Shelley at her Website
www.shelleymunro.com

Join Shelley's Newsletter
www.shelleymunro.com/newsletter

Follow Shelley at Bookbub
www.bookbub.com/authors/shelley-munro

ALSO BY SHELLEY

Sports Romances
No Defense
Best Man
Eye on the Ball

Paranormal Romances
Curse Across Time
Lone Wolf
Seeking Kokopelli
Last Wish
Fallen Idol
My Stray Cat
My Cat Nap

SHELLEY MUNRO

Paranormal Box Set
Under His Spell